Poverty

David M. Haugen and Matthew J. Box, Book Editors

Bruce Glassman, Vice President
Bonnie Szumski, Publisher
Helen Cothran, Managing Editor
Scott Barbour, Series Editor

GREENHAVEN PRESS
An imprint of Thomson Gale, a part of The Thomson Corporation

THOMSON
GALE

Detroit • New York • San Francisco • San Diego • New Haven, Conn.
Waterville, Maine • London • Munich

For more information, contact
Greenhaven Press
27500 Drake Rd.
Farmington Hills, MI 48331-3535
Or you can visit our Internet site at http://www.gale.com

Cover credit: © Nathan Benn/CORBIS. Children play outside tenement housing in a small town in Vermont where unemployment is high due to the decline in industrial jobs.

LIBRARY OF CONGRESS CATALOGING-IN-PUBLICATION DATA

Poverty / David M. Haugen and Matthew J. Box, book editors.
   p. cm. — (Social issues firsthand)
Includes bibliographical references and index.
ISBN 0-7377-2899-X (lib. : alk. paper)
   1. Homelessness—United States. 2. Working class—United States. 3. Poor—United States. 4. Poverty—United States—Prevention. I. Haugen, David M., 1969– . II. Box, Matthew J. III. Series.
HV4505.P678   2006
362.5'0973—dc22   2005045120

CONTENTS

viewer how she shoplifts to provide her family with the
things they need and desire.

tence in her native land only to find that a lack of opportunities in the United States forces her to return to subsistence labor.

CHAPTER 4: HELPING THE POOR

Social issues are often viewed in abstract terms. Pressing challenges such as poverty, homelessness, and addiction are viewed as problems to be defined and solved. Politicians, social scientists, and other experts engage in debates about the extent of the problems, their causes, and how best to remedy them. Often overlooked in these discussions is the human dimension of the issue. Behind every policy debate over poverty, homelessness, and substance abuse, for example, are real people struggling to make ends meet, to survive life on the streets, and to overcome addiction to drugs and alcohol. Their stories are ubiquitous and compelling. They are the stories of everyday people—perhaps your own family members or friends—and yet they rarely influence the debates taking place in state capitols, the national Congress, or the courts.

The disparity between the public debate and private experience of social issues is well illustrated by looking at the topic of poverty. Each year the U.S. Census Bureau establishes a poverty threshold. A household with an income below the threshold is defined as poor, while a household with an income above the threshold is considered able to live on a basic subsistence level. For example, in 2003 a family of two was considered poor if its income was less than $12,015; a family of four was defined as poor if its income was less than $18,810. Based on this system, the bureau estimates that 35.9 million Americans (12.5 percent of the population) lived below the poverty line in 2003, including 12.9 million children below the age of eighteen.

Commentators disagree about what these statistics mean. Social activists insist that the huge number of officially poor Americans translates into human suffering. Even many families that have incomes above the threshold, they maintain, are likely to be struggling to get by. Other commentators insist that the statistics exaggerate the problem of poverty in the United States. Compared to people in developing countries, they point out, most so-called poor families have a high quality of life. As stated by journalist Fidelis Iyebote, "Cars are owned by 70 percent of 'poor' households. . . . Color televisions belong to 97 percent of the 'poor' [and] videocassette recorders belong to nearly 75 percent. . . . Sixty-four percent have microwave ovens, half own a stereo system, and over a quarter possess an automatic dishwasher."

However, this debate over the poverty threshold and what it means is likely irrelevant to a person living in poverty. Simply put, poor people do not need the government to tell them whether they are poor. They can see it in the stack of bills they cannot pay. They are aware of it when they are forced to choose between paying rent or buying food for their children. They become painfully conscious of it when they lose their homes and are forced to live in their cars or on the streets. Indeed, the written stories of poor people define the meaning of poverty more vividly than a government bureaucracy could ever hope to. Narratives composed by the poor describe losing jobs due to injury or mental illness, depict horrific tales of childhood abuse and spousal violence, recount the loss of friends and family members. They evoke the slipping away of social supports and government assistance, the descent into substance abuse and addiction, the harsh realities of life on the streets. These are the perspectives on poverty that are too often omitted from discussions over the extent of the problem and how to solve it.

Greenhaven Press's Social Issues Firsthand series provides a forum for the often-overlooked human perspectives on society's most divisive topics of debate. Each volume focuses on one social issue and presents a collection of ten to sixteen narratives by those who have had personal involvement with the topic. Extra care has been taken to include a diverse range of perspectives. For example, in the volume on adoption, readers will find the stories of birth parents who have given up their children for adoption, adoptive parents, and adoptees themselves. After exposure to these varied points of view, the reader will have a clearer understanding that adoption is an intense, emotional experience full of joyous highs and painful lows for all concerned.

Each book in the series contains several features that enhance its usefulness, including an in-depth introduction, an annotated table of contents, bibliographies for further research, a list of organizations to contact, and a thorough index. These elements—combined with the poignant voices of people touched by tragedy and triumph—make the Social Issues Firsthand series a valuable resource for research on today's topics of political discussion.

The Controversial Scope of Poverty in America

The U.S. Census Bureau computes poverty by taking into account the number of wage earners and the number of dependent children in a family (a single person is considered a family in this case) and then assigning that family a "threshold" level of income. For example, according to the 2004 census, the national poverty-threshold income for a family of four (with two adults and two children) was $19,157. Similarly, a family of six (with two adults and 4 children) required more than $25,241 to remain above the poverty line. Since these numbers reflect national averages, some families may have needed more or less money to survive poverty, depending on the cost of living in their region of the country.

Poverty thresholds create black-and-white divisions. Families that possess a total income below their respective income threshold are considered living in poverty. Those that earn even a few dollars more than the threshold are believed not to be impoverished. The Census Bureau acknowledges that this measure is not precise, stating that thresholds "are intended for use as a statistical yardstick, not as a complete description of what people and families need to live."[1] The bureau also recognizes that these measures do not take into account the varying degrees of poverty that exist below a threshold. Thus, a family with an income just under their poverty threshold is not likely to be living in destitution, yet the family members may not be able to set money aside for college funds, retirement needs, or some necessities. Conversely, a family with an income slightly above the threshold may have similar struggles. According to the Census Bureau, the poverty index is merely a statistical means of keeping track of the financial health of the American people.

The 2004 census (using data gleaned from 2003) revealed that poverty levels rose in the United States from 12.1 percent in 2002 to 12.5 percent in 2003. An additional 1.3 million people joined the ranks of the poor in 2003, bringing the national total to 35.9 million

Americans. The rise in poverty occurred despite the fact that the average national family income remained unchanged at around forty-three thousand dollars.

THE DEMOGRAPHICS OF POVERTY

Census Bureau indexes show that poverty has increased primarily within certain demographic categories. Women, for example, experienced a decline in wages by more than half a percent—a phenomenon that has not occurred since 1995. (Men's income remained unchanged from 2002.) In addition, the number of children living in poverty increased from 12.1 million in 2002 to 12.9 million in 2003. Racial and ethnic factors were also at play in the poverty statistics. Asian Americans saw a relatively small increase (1.7 percent) in poverty levels. Hispanics living in America, on the other hand, showed the greatest increases in poverty because the population of Hispanics grew rapidly (aided by an influx of illegal immigrants). The number of Hispanics living in poverty rose from 8.6 million in 2002 to 9.1 million in 2003. This means that the median income of Hispanics dropped 2.6 percent during that interval. Blacks, whites, and other minority groups did not experience any significant change in poverty levels from 2002.

The average household income did not fluctuate in most sections of the country, but the South did witness a 1.5 percent drop in median income. In fact, Arkansas, Louisiana, Mississippi, and West Virginia were four of the five states with the highest percentage (18.5 percent) of poverty over a three-year period (2001–2003).

DIRE PREDICTIONS

While the Census Bureau maintains all of these numbers to chart the rise and decline of poverty in America, the bureau is not a policy-making body, and therefore it makes few claims outside of its statistical purview. For example, the most partisan statement made by the Census Bureau in 2004 was that the 2003–2004 poverty rate remained "below the average of the 1980s and 1990s"[2] when the country was plagued by recession. Since the census figures are so clear-cut, while the issues that surround poverty are not, it is the politicians and pundits of all stripes who interpret census data to support their own policy agendas.

Some contend that living in poverty translates into real hardships. These include reduced access to health care and adequate food. As the Census Bureau reports, more than 243 million people in America lacked health insurance in 2003; this number had grown by a million from the previous year. Some critics attribute the rise in uninsured to the unwillingness of many companies hurt by recession to include or expand health benefits as part of employment. In addition, the U.S. Department of Agriculture released statistics that claimed 11 percent of American households lacked adequate, healthy food sometime in the year, and this number has increased from 2001. Of these "food insecure," as the government calls them, 3.8 million were chronically hungry. As a result, many U.S. cities called upon emergency food relief from government storehouses to abate the problem.

Those who believe that the census figures paint a dire picture of America's well-being suggest that society is being increasingly divided along the lines of rich and poor. According to *CNN/Money* staff writer Octavio Blanco, "The growth in the number of poor should give us pause, but even more troubling is the growing disparity in America between who is rich and who is poor."[3] Observers argue that stocks and investments are bolstering the gains of the wealthy, while those who lack such securities are struggling simply to find jobs. Some worry that this disparity is being masked by the overall economic recovery of the nation. As Peter Grier and Patrik Jonsson wryly note in the January 2004 issue of the *Christian Science Monitor*, "Big-screen TVs are blowing out the doors of retailers, but 34 million Americans still live below the poverty line. The US GDP [gross domestic product, a statistical indicator of production income] is roaring ahead, but the nation still has the worst child-poverty rate in the industrialized world."[4]

Others argue that politicians are downplaying the census findings in order to promote the image of a robust America that focuses on middle-class consumer power. One editorial in the *San Jose Mercury News* in November 2004 lamented the fact that poverty was not even an issue in the presidential election campaign of that year. According to the author, both the Democratic and Republican platforms catered to the middle class and ignored the poor because "the poor aren't classified as likely voters, and they don't contribute to political campaigns."[5] The editorial goes on to assert that America's middle class even frets over the cost of social service programs and hopes that bare minimum contributions will compel the poor to help themselves out of their plight.

Not all assessments of poverty in America, however, support such a baleful outlook. Robert E. Rector and Kirk A. Johnson, two analysts with the Heritage Foundation, a conservative research and policy organization, have tried to separate the notion of living below the Census Bureau poverty line from the commonly held stereotype that poverty equates to destitution. According to Rector and Johnson,

> Overall, the typical American defined as poor by the government has a car, air conditioning, a refrigerator, a stove, a clothes washer and dryer, and a microwave. He has two color televisions, cable or satellite TV reception, a VCR or DVD player, and a stereo. He is able to obtain medical care. His home is in good repair and is not overcrowded. By his own report, his family is not hungry and he had sufficient funds in the past year to meet his family's essential needs. While this individual's life is not opulent, it is equally far from the popular images of dire poverty conveyed by the press, liberal activists, and politicians.[6]

Rector and Johnson specifically reject the argument that poor Americans lack adequate food: "America's poor are far from being chronically undernourished. The average consumption of protein, vitamins, and minerals is virtually the same for poor and middle-class children and, in most cases, is well above recommended norms."[7]

There are poor people in America, Rector and Johnson concede, but very few of them lack shelter, nutritious food, or a car (among other modern conveniences). The majority are merely working folks who may not live in splendor but certainly do not live in want.

Others reject the claim that the poor lack sufficient health care. Alan Reynolds, a senior member of the libertarian Cato Institute, states, "Going without health insurance is not the same as going without health care." In fact, Reynolds maintains, "The uninsured are not generally poor—if they were, they would qualify for Medicaid (aside from new immigrants, especially illegal immigrants, who account for most low-income uninsured). A third of the uninsured have household incomes above $50,000." Reynolds argues that liberal advocates often use large numbers—such as the 243 million uninsured Americans—to make grand, yet unsubstantiated, claims about poverty. Merely looking at the poverty rate, however, tells a different story to Reynolds. By comparing the 2003 census statistics with those of 1998, Reynolds notes, "The percentage of Americans living in poverty was 12.5 percent [in 2003], 12.7 percent in 1998. The percentage without health insurance was 15.6 percent [in 2003], 16.3 percent in 1998."[8] Reynolds and others have asserted that the

Census Bureau's poverty rate has risen only slightly in the new millennium but has remained far below the 13.9 percent average for the years 1980 to 1998 (and remains lower than the rate of any single year within that range). From this perspective, poverty in America has not been eliminated, but it has remained comparatively low and does not suggest a deteriorating economy or a divided nation.

While much of the poverty debate is being waged by economists and policy makers, those struggling to make ends meet often go unheard. In the following anthology of personal narratives, the impoverished and their advocates detail what it is like to be poor in America at the end of the twentieth century and the beginning of the twenty-first. The poor among these unappointed spokespersons speak of how their daily routines are always determined by their lack of conveniences and necessities. Their plight is one of survival, and their trials are far removed from the dry census statistics that inform the political debates over how serious the problem of poverty is in the United States.

NOTES

1. U.S. Census Bureau, "How the Census Bureau Measures Poverty," www.census.gov/hhes/poverty/povdef.html.
2. U.S. Census Bureau, press release, August 26, 2004. www.census.gov/Press-Release/www/releases/archives/income_wealth/002484.html.
3. Octavio Blanco, "The Changing Face of Poverty: Millions of Americans Live in Poverty, More Families Are Suffering and Hunger Is Seen Growing," *CNN/Money Online*, December 30, 2004. http://money.cnn.com/2004/12/22/news/economy/poverty_overview.
4. Peter Grier and Patrik Jonsson, "In War on Poverty, Early Gains and a Long Stalemate," *Christian Science Monitor*, January 9, 2004.
5. *San Jose* (California) *Mercury News*, "The Poor: Unseen and Ignored," November 2, 2004.
6. Robert E. Rector and Kirk A. Johnson, "Understanding Poverty in America," Heritage Foundation, January 5, 2004. www.heritage.org/Research/Welfare/bg1713.cfm.
7. Rector and Johnson, "Understanding Poverty in America."
8. Alan Reynolds, "Recalling the 1998 Tumble," Cato Institute, September 15, 2004. www.cato.org/pub_display.php?pub_id=2820.

CHAPTER 1

Homelessness

A Homeless Vet Categorizes the Homeless

by Tom Musselwhite

Tom Musselwhite, a Vietnam veteran with a disabling leg injury, became homeless in 1992 after his workers' compensation application was denied. Within a year, Musselwhite used the information he had gathered on homelessness as well as his own experiences of living on the streets of Eugene, Oregon, to become a spokesperson for the state's homeless population. He has since served as the editor of *'oIkos*, a newspaper published by Project Recover, an organization that aids the homeless and impoverished citizens of the Eugene area. Now living in a twelve-foot trailer, Musselwhite has shelter, but he still lives a rootless existence that prompts him to continue advocating for the homeless.

In the following article, Musselwhite explains that the homeless residents of his state are not a homogeneous group: Many are mentally ill, some are drug abusers, and others have just fallen on hard times. What connects them all, however, is that they live in abject poverty without the sympathy of the government or the average citizen.

I am a 49-year-old father of three, Vietnam era U.S. Navy veteran. Raised in a large, old-fashioned extended family in the Deep South, I was brought up with a strong work ethic. I have worked for my living since the age of twelve. I graduated high school and have two years of college. I have lived in Oregon for over twenty years.

In late 1992, the onset of a disabling leg condition prevented me from continuing my career as a pre-press technician in the printing industry. Coupled with stresses I had carried since the Vietnam years, I hit a wall of sorts.

My workers' comp claim was denied because the state had recently enacted legislation disallowing preexisting conditions and I admitted to having pulled a muscle as a teenager.

Tom Musselwhite, "Homelessness in Oregon: Life on the Streets," http://eesc.orst.edu.

LIVING ON THE STREETS

I spent the next two years living in a $200, 1965 Ford van on the streets of Eugene. No income, unable to perform regular physical labor, unable to professionally employ the skills I had developed, then denied Veterans benefits, I was also too proud to stand in line for food, handouts, or jump through the system's hoops designed to weed out fraud. By late 1993 I had become active in the Homeless Action Coalition and was making myself a regular presence at city hall.

Technically, I am still homeless, but thanks to a new law enacted by the city of Eugene I can live in a 12-foot travel trailer parked in the backyard of a local nonprofit.

Although my situation was dire enough, I think what bothered me most was seeing so many others who had simply lost all hope with no way out short of a miracle.

The following is based on my own experience, not particularly scientific, but generally confirmed by the research of others and myself.

HOMELESSNESS AND MENTAL ILLNESS

Of the most visible "on the street" homeless, about one-third or perhaps up to fifty percent, are suffering from mental illness.

Most authorities agree that of the mentally ill homeless, about half become homeless as a result of an existing mental illness, the other half become mentally ill as a result of becoming homeless. It is, after all, no small obstacle when your life circumstances change so dramatically that you suddenly find yourself without a bed, bathroom, cooking facilities, and forbidden by authorities to protect yourself from the elements or even sit down and rest. I have witnessed far too many instances of people walking around in the rain all night; some wrapped in a wet blanket for protection, some with a raincoat or umbrella, some with no protection at all. I have seen people banging their heads against telephone poles as if looking for a distraction from their misfortune, and some just walking around and around in tiny circles mumbling to themselves.

HOMELESSNESS AND CHEMICAL DEPENDENCE

Another third of the most visible "on the street" sort have drug or alcohol dependencies. Like the mentally ill population, sometimes it is easy to believe that as many as fifty percent of the population we are talking about have a primary drug or alcohol problem.

These two populations tend to overlap each other. The dually diagnosed are those who are diagnosed with both a disabling mental illness and a substance abuse problem.

HOMELESS VETERANS

So far we have categorized, with a broad brush, sixty to seventy-five percent of the most visible of the homeless we see on our streets. Who are the other, more or less, thirty percent?

The Department of Veterans Affairs maintains that one-third of all homeless are veterans. Many homeless vets have also developed substance abuse problems and some are mentally ill.

WHO ARE THE REST?

That leaves about twenty percent of our "most visible homeless" to sort into groups we can comfortably cubbyhole. Who are they?

Until recently, I felt rather comfortable with the above figures. I would have concluded by saying the balance of the homeless were:

• the disabled and elderly-retired who are unable to increase their incomes and have been priced out of the housing market, sometimes due to the cost of medicines needed for their health;

• older single males estranged from families or with no families;

• an increasing number of females, those with few skills, poorly educated, or simply disadvantaged by nature.

Most are caught in an economic situation where they simply are not competitive in the job market and therefore are unable to consistently maintain housing in an increasingly expensive housing market.

Larger in number, another segment of the "homeless" are called the "hidden homeless." The "hidden homeless" are those doubled up with friends, family, or otherwise comfortably out of sight.

Today I am not so comfortable with that conclusion. Today I am confronted by more and more families, even just children on the street with no place to stay and a far cry from having any place to call home.

And what do they endure? Not just predation from drug dealers and an underground sex market, but also abuse by the very policing authorities which had-oughta-be protecting *all* of us.

They are doused with gasoline and set on fire. Awakened in the middle of the night by vicious gangs and beaten, raped, tortured, or murdered. They are run down and run over by people driving vehicles, and chased away from commercial districts by profit-minded entrepreneurs. Even the religious organizations whose duty it is to provide relief to the unfortunate are often forbidden to do so, even if they wanted to.

Now that we have sorted and characterized the "most visible homeless" let us ask what common feature they share? It is not chronic alcoholism, drug abuse, or mental illness.

The common thread between all is poverty.

A Homeless Activist Fights to Change Public Attitudes

by David R. Quammen

> In the following narrative, David R. Quammen describes his up-
> bringing in South Dakota during the post–World War II years,
> noting specifically how he and his family managed to live con-
> tently while surviving on a low income. As Quammen grew up,
> however, the childhood contentment disappeared when his first
> two marriages failed, he took to bouts of heavy drinking, and his
> finances became unstable. After his first business failed in 1983,
> Quammen became homeless in California. He recovered for a
> short time, but various economic ups and downs led him back to
> homelessness in the next decade.
>
> His rough experiences turned Quammen into an advocate
> for the poor. Penning a document on what he perceived as the
> shameless way in which the state of California treated its im-
> poverished and homeless populations, Quammen began a mail-
> ing campaign to elicit the support of any official who would lis-
> ten. Not receiving any positive responses, Quammen continued
> unabated to try to get his message out. He eventually created
> Project Restore Hope in America, an advocacy agency in Wash-
> ington, D.C., and has since taken his complaints about the na-
> tion's treatment of the poor to the Internet. Quammen hopes
> that his struggle will lead not to handouts but to serious efforts
> by the government and private organizations to help the poor
> help themselves out of their predicament.

My interest in poverty is deep rooted, influenced by my upbringing in a small South Dakota town in the forties and the events
from then until becoming homeless for the second time on March
15th, 1993, after which I made the decision to actively pursue
changes in how we treat our poor.

David R. Quammen, "One Man's Poverty: A Personal Story," *The Sticky Wicket: Poverty's Home Page,* www2.ari.net/home/poverty, April 6, 1996. Copyright © 1996 by David R. Quammen. Reproduced by permission.

Born in 1939 in the closing days of the Great Depression, separated by two years from an older sister and a younger brother, my parents struggled like the rest of the country to build a life for their young family as the world became engulfed in the great conflict of World War II.

SELF-RELIANCE DURING THE WAR YEARS

My first enduring memory is of living in two refurbished rooms of a burned out two story house near my grandparents in 1944 while my father fought in Europe, spending most of his Army career as a German POW in a camp the name of which I can't remember, it and much of the remaining evidence of my past lost during my latest encounter with homelessness.

The innocence of youth masked our circumstance, which improved along with the rest of the nation as the post war recovery brought new wealth and prosperity to those able and willing to take part in this rebirth. For me, that included a Sunday morning paper route in the fifth grade, adding a daily route the following year, keeping both until dropping the Sunday chore sometime in the eighth grade.

My father and his best friend, the father of my best friend, added to our growing home while my mother added to the family income through her position as a teacher in a one room rural schoolhouse serving the outlying farming community. Most of our diet was satisfied by the large garden that provided fresh sustenance during the summer, the remaining months sustained from the canned and preserved fruits of our labor.

The thirty-or-so dollar a month pay from my seven day a week jobs was divided between frivolities and necessities, much of it going to a clothing budget that added to a meager closet filled with home made shirts and the more functional surprises under the Christmas tree each year.

My mother was a firm believer in self-reliance, acquiring this trait following the death of her own mother when mine was thirteen, earning teaching credentials through her labors as a young woman, and the difficult task of working to provide for us during the war years. She sought to impart this to us by giving responsibility and the freedom to exercise that gift through our own choices. More than once, she said of others "They made their bed, let them lie in it."

The paper routes provided more than money, allowing me to observe the variety of lifestyles of those I served, ranging from the more well off to one large family in particular, their many ill clothed children born in the ramshackle house. Yet even with that, their generosity showed at Christmas with a small gift, more than once offering to share ice cream on a hot summer day as I trudged the several miles assigned me.

Other things like the comment an across-the-street neighbor about my age, ten, or so, made when my mother called the city to have weeds cut in their yard—"Your mother doesn't like us because we're poor,"—didn't affect me then like it does now.

Less than a block away, remnants of a once thriving Hobo Jungle next to the railroad track that cut a path through our neighborhood still showed periodic debris of recent visitors who had warmed themselves by a fire that also served to provide a hot meal, as evidenced by the sooted tin cans scattered around the occasionally warm pile of charred twigs and branches.

Then there's Rosie Redwing. I never knew her well, can't even remember talking to her, but everyone in Junior High knew she lived in the abandoned bus on the edge of town, those delicate matters of life served by a discarded auto a few feet away.

THE VEIL OF YOUTHFUL INNOCENCE IS LIFTED

The innocence of youth gets peeled away as we grow up, gradually separating us from our fellow man, guided by a mentality that says what we have is who we are. That point hit home in my Junior year in High School when the man I worked for drove me on a search for a kid I thought I saw take something from the store he managed. His first reaction was to cruise a poor section of town, commenting as we turned a corner near a friend's home "We're among 'em now," as though this were the only place in town a prospective thief might be.

These things went against the grain of my Lutheran teaching, that of love and concern for others regardless of their situation, more so for me since from a young age I aspired to bring this love to those not so fortunate to be exposed to what I held so dear. Time heals, but also can diminish youthful ambitions in favor of the grander trappings of a more material nature. I succumbed to this as I reflected on what was denied me in my early years.

There wasn't money for college and my part time job that supplied minor typewriter repair skills vanished when my boss's business failed, so an unplanned trip to the recruiter's office with a friend led to high scores on the tests taken to pass the time while he took his, then to a train ride to the Naval Training Center in San Diego. This, in turn, led to Aviation Electronics training in Memphis, then to assignments in Mountain View, California, where I later met and married my first wife.

California held the promise of the future with the beginnings of the young semiconductor industry, enhanced by a blossoming junior college system that made higher learning accessible to lean budgets, if one so desired. I desired and pursued it with vigor until sometime after our second child and an introduction to the after-work carousing with those who had already been conferred with that status symbol that separates the learned from the rest. Our third child came even as it became more clear that the vows of forever more were too hastily declared.

A second marriage and another child fell to the wayside for other reasons, leading to financial hardships worsened by cyclical changes in the economy, exacerbated by heavy drinking that seemed to soothe the resentments of seeing others less capable than I succeed more from the degrees they had acquired than from their accomplishments in a fickle industry. The inescapable result was involuntary termination following major surgery that diminished physical endurance, but strengthened my resolve to achieve on my own what was withheld by others.

RECESSION IN THE EIGHTIES CAUSES A STRUGGLE

This new spirit led to a number of successes which were hampered by the back-to-back recessions of the early eighties, adding weight to the task of trying through two years of psychiatric counseling to relieve myself from the burden that alcohol posed to my future.

My first bout with homelessness began in late 1983, then a twist of fate brought me to a program that led me to a sober existence, allowing me to grow spiritually and financially with a renewed resolve to make a contribution to whatever community I may be a member of. The glitter that became Silicon Valley was dampened by the overcrowding of success, so I turned my sights to more peaceful surroundings in search of a challenge worthy of my newfound confidence.

My nature is to believe in people until proven otherwise, a failing that cost me all I had gained when the individual I formed a business with failed to move, as promised, resigning from the corporation after my initial investment, borrowed against an almost paid for home in the San Francisco Bay Area, ran out. I persevered against all odds for three years until the failing business had consumed all but a few of my possessions.

In the meantime, I had organized the other manufacturers in the small community that became my home into an organization that, to me, was an important tool for the future growth of manufacturing in that area, serving as president the first two years. During that period, I devoted perhaps too much time and effort in building relationships with the local business, education and government entities to enhance the potential I saw to serve the larger Northern California manufacturing operations.

When I closed the doors of the manufacturing business, the other members of the association closed their doors on me, perhaps as much from the aggressive nature of my pursuits in that organization as from their perception that during these troubled times, I had turned to drugs, something completely unfounded, yet given my behavior during my fall, perhaps justifiable in their eyes.

I was able to buy an auto body and paint business through a lease arrangement, which I took over in June of 1990 within days of closing the manufacturing company. My previous experience and interest in classic cars justified that move, but the recession that began the following month doomed it to failure within eleven months, leaving less than a hundred dollar debt to the leasing company, but adding to the operating debt burden owed from the manufacturing business.

The ensuing two years were hard, seldom having money for basics, eventually leading to relying on a friend for shelter. He lost his job to the recession, eventually losing his home to foreclosure, at which point my own options gave out, leaving me homeless. During the final months of that period, I continued to explore whatever possibilities might exist for my own future, turning to a variation in small scale farming that I had been toying with for more than a decade.

FROM POVERTY TO ACTIVISM

As the plan evolved, I began to see in it the potential to do more than just to satisfy personal needs. My own exposure to poverty, whether personally affected by it or observing its affect on others, and the continuing loss of opportunity and lack of concern by those in a position of authority coupled with the way I had been treated during my own recent downfall instilled an anger in me that grew as local politicians and community leaders failed to provide affordable housing for the poor, and instead, added to their burden by imposing fees and charges that had an unconscionably detrimental impact on those whose basic existence was threatened by the worsening economy.

As the plan neared completion, this anger became more and more a part of what otherwise should have been a document to elicit support for a promising business venture. Perhaps as much of what was expressed in it was to vent my own feelings of disgust as it was an attempt to let others see the callous and inequitable treatment of our nation's poor. It became immaterial to me whether or not that would jeopardize the plan, since it seemed that the larger problem was in fact a genuine ignorance of the effects of what political and business leaders do in pursuit of profits and balanced budgets.

I prefer to believe it is ignorance, not malice, that moves people to behave in such an irresponsible manner, for it seems easier to enlighten the ignorant than to soften the malicious. Whatever the case, it has become an all-consuming passion, and given my background and the renewed inspiration of my childhood faith, it gives me back an ambition I once held in high esteem.

The document, for I know not what else to call it, was completed on January 14th, 1993, whereupon I began mailing copies to any I could think of. The first included California Gov. Pete Wilson, Mr. Jimmy Carter, Mr. Ross Perot, then president-elect Bill Clinton and two people in my community I respected and admired.

The list expanded to Senator Daniel Moynihan, Cal State Sen. Dan McCorquodale, Cal Assemblywoman Margaret Snyder, Senator Dianne Feinstein and a number of others in various positions of authority or responsibility that either came to mind, or were identified in the media as involved in dealing with poverty in one way or other.

What few responses came back were either non-responsive (California State Homeless Coordinator), or simply acknowledged receipt (Pres. Bill Clinton). I responded with additional correspondence, but in truth, I knew that it would not generate the interest I was after.

In considering my next move, I made a decision on March 8th while doing my laundry in preparation for my then-impending homelessness that, since I would be homeless anyway, I would go to Washington to pursue support personally. I made arrangements with a local charitable group for some food, a haircut and a pair of shoes, called the editor of the local newspaper and set Monday, March 15th, to leave, which I did.

Even with trouble with my 1972 VW Van and a two day visit with my younger son in Oklahoma, I made it to Manassas, just outside DC, at midnight, Sunday, the 21st. On the 22nd, I met a man while attempting to contact Sen. Feinstein's office, and after reading the sign on my van—"I'm taking a plan to the President that can help Homeless Americans help themselves—project Restore Hope In America"—he decided to help me. That evolved into an arrangement whereby I would do work on a dilapidated historic building in the city's Shaw District in exchange for a place to stay, which also required refurbishing. The building had housed the first Black Music Conservatory in the country.

CHANGING PUBLIC ATTITUDES

While trying to gain support for my plan, I modified the basic concept to suit conditions in Shaw and incorporated the nonprofit group, Restore Hope In America, on August 30, 1993. I knew that for anything meaningful to happen, public opinion about the poor would have to change, so I wrote a piece, "It's Homeless Out Tonight," to introduce the group and sent it to over thirty members of the media. Ms. P.J. Robinson, contributing editor of the *Metro Herald* in Alexandria, VA, was the only one interested. The piece was published on October 22, 1993.

In December, I approached her about submitting something on a regular basis, whereupon she told me to submit a few things and "We'll see." Two articles in December were well received, opening the door for a weekly column, which began on January 7, 1994, and continues today. I have used it as a platform to stimulate interest in my plan, which was formally introduced on June 24, 1994, to attack those who attack the poor and to present alternate views of both why we have so many poor and the true nature of their bleak existence.

In June of 1995, I expanded my efforts to include The Sticky Wicket: Poverty's Home Page, on the Internet, hoping to use it to share ideas with others working toward helping the poor. It is my firm belief that the greatest problem facing the vast majority of America's able-bodied poor is that they are excluded from participating in the mainstream economy in any meaningful way. The plan of self-help which evolved from my original concept addresses this issue specifically, and if implemented, can lead to economic independence for those who are truly interested in helping themselves.

REFINING THE SOCIAL IMAGE OF POVERTY

While I am concerned about all those in poverty, my focus is on the able-bodied poor, since very little of our resources are dedicated to helping them to help themselves. For a variety of reasons, few of them valid, some even dishonest, we, as a society, have a tendency to do things FOR the poor, rather than provide them with the means to help themselves. The current welfare debates are founded more on false stereotypes and self-serving political rhetoric, and as such, have resulted in proposed legislation, both federal and state, that will penalize the poor for things largely not their fault. Conservative efforts are punitive in nature, and liberal attempts at help are inept and fail utterly at delivering real help so that the poor might become self sufficient.

Of even greater distress is that this same attitude about the poor extends into many groups which are at the forefront of helping the poor. I have been openly critical of community development corporations around the country who receive tens of billions of dollars to "revitalize" poor communities, yet they give the jobs and the opportunities created in the name of renewal to outsiders, rather than to the able-bodied poor in the neighborhoods in which they do their so-called good works, this even as they openly acknowledge that jobs and economic opportunity are what the poor in these communities need the most.

POOR BY CHOICE

These, and a variety of other concerns about how we treat our poor, are scattered about in my website, along with numerous recommendations on more appropriate plans of self-help that lead to economic independence. I live in poverty now by choice, sustaining myself and my efforts by doing janitorial and menial tasks. This not only allows me to devote more time to my plan of self-help, it also keeps me focused on the economic and social injustices inflicted on our poor, as a class.

And even though I have worked hard to keep my end of the bargain in the various arrangements which I've been able to make to sustain myself, there have been several set-backs from causes beyond my control, the most recent when I effectively—and illegally—evicted a drug gang from the building where I live, an action which resulted in a death threat against me and severely hindered my ability to earn money.

At this point in my life, however, I can think of nothing better to do with myself than to continue the course I have charted, for it seems clear to me that until we change our attitude about the poor and what we do about their circumstances, millions of poor Americans will continue to languish needlessly in an environment which will only cause greater chaos and turmoil for all in our society. In far too many ways, we are not what we say we are, and until we begin to deal honestly with our poor, we will fall far short of the ideals and the values which we espouse.

This is the greatest nation in the world today, but there has never been, nor will there ever be, a society that cannot improve upon itself. We owe it to our heritage and to our future to act now. Failure to do so would denigrate everything we stand for, and that would disgrace us all.

Suffering in the Shelter

by Judy Ann Eichstedt

Judy Ann Eichstedt is a poet and activist in Tulsa, Oklahoma.
Though she now has a home for her six children, she spent
roughly five years in dire poverty. At the height of her financial
troubles, Eichstedt's husband had to take the kids and travel to
search for work. Eichstedt was left behind to eke out an existence on the street. In the following narrative, Eichstedt describes what led her family to poverty and what her life was like
when she was abandoned. As Eichstedt relates, her pride initially
kept her from seeking refuge in a homeless shelter, but after having "nowhere else to go," she eventually took advantage of social
services. Eichstedt's experience in the shelter system, though
temporary, was heartbreaking, as she illustrates. Eichstedt luck-
ily found work that helped her get back on her feet, but she never
forgot the haunting memories of her nights in the shelter.

I have slept in cars, under bridges, in homeless shelters, and in
abandoned buildings. I know what it's like to be on the streets
with my husband and our six children. I also know how it feels to be
homeless and alone.

Our family spent almost five years going back and forth from
poor and barely making it to homeless and living on the streets. We
spent several months living out of our worn-down battered car, traveling not only from city to city but from state to state, trying to find
work and a place to belong. We learned to expect the odd looks
from people who would see us sleeping in a rest area when we were
too tired to go on. But when people would laugh at us (as if there is
something funny about being homeless), it cut deep into our hearts.

As my husband looked for work, my children and I would spend
hours walking up and down the streets, collecting cans to return for
deposit. Cars would rush by as if we weren't even there. On a good
day, we would find enough cans to get bread, bologna, and something to drink.

Judy Ann Eichstedt, "The Cry of Poverty," *The Other Side*, vol. 37, July 2001, p. 26. Copyright © 2001 by *The Other Side*. Reproduced by permission.

HARD TIMES

When my husband would return in the evening with news that he hadn't found work, it was hard to hang on to hope—let alone have faith that tomorrow might be a bit better. When a potential employer hears that you have no home address or phone, you're shown the door quickly. Going to a job interview in clothes you've slept in gives you little chance. People assume that anyone who is homeless is a drunk, an addict, or guilty of some crime. There's nothing you can do to change their minds.

Sometimes my husband would stand by the road with a sign that said "Will work for food." If I could, I would join him, since people tended to be more compassionate when a woman was standing there, too. Still, people would drive by and yell horrible names at us, throw their drinks on us, or shout "Get off the streets!" A few times, people spit right in our faces.

We often found our breakfast in the garbage cans behind a grocery store. On a good day, we'd be lucky enough to find some moldy bread and a few bruised and dirty apples or bananas. Occasionally, a store manager would come out and chase us off, threatening to call the police. Ashamed and embarrassed, we would hurry away, disappearing again into the darkness of homelessness.

PRAYING FOR RELIEF

When it all seemed impossible to cope with, I would often pray to God for strength to carry on. By flashlight at night, I'd read my Bible, searching for an answer—not only for us, but for all who are poor. Why are we who are poor or homeless treated as if we were evil? Why are our cries ignored and our suffering taken so lightly? Why do people seem to feel we can be thrown away and forgotten? One night, I came to the story in Matthew's Gospel where a young man asks Jesus what he must do to find eternal life. Jesus reminds him that he must keep the commandments; "This I have done," the young man responds.

"Go sell all you have and give it to the poor," Jesus says. Reading these words, I realized that, in spite of all my pain of homelessness and hunger, Jesus had not forgotten me. Jesus cares greatly about those who are poor like me—and about our sufferings. In his eyes, I am not the broken, beaten-down, poor person the world sees. To him, I am precious.

GOING TO A HOMELESS SHELTER

I spent many nights on the streets before I ever set foot inside a homeless shelter. But I'll never forget my first time there.

At the time, I was living alone. Poverty has a way of ruining everything, and my relationship with my husband had fallen apart due to the stress of continually living on the edge. He had gone with our children to another state in search of work, and I was living on the streets.

No one wants to go to a shelter, but I was at the end of my rope. The large brick building seemed threatening as I approached, and I thought of turning away. "You have nowhere else to go," I reminded myself, and stepped inside.

There, I came face to face with all the people society views as disposable. I was amazed to see so many children and elderly folks. There was a baby that could not have been more than a few weeks old. It broke my heart to see the pain of all these forgotten people. I remember being overwhelmed by the sheer number of people who had ended up there. If all these people aren't able to make it on their own, I thought, how do I stand a chance?

I desperately wanted to run out the door. But I fought back the tears, swallowed what was left of my pride, and went into the social worker's office. She offered me a seat without looking up from her newspaper.

"Do you have any money?" she asked.

"No." I was tempted to tell her that if I had money, I would go to the Holiday Inn, not a shelter—but of course, I didn't.

She asked if I had family I could stay with. Didn't she realize that I would never have been there, answering questions that were not only personal but embarrassing, if I had family that would take me in? So many of my friends and family had turned their backs on me when I became homeless, a fact that still haunts me deeply. It wasn't easy to share my deepest sorrows with this stranger.

After a few more questions, she told me the rules—no drinking, no drugs, no fighting, and so forth. I assured her I would cause no trouble. I was given a blanket and a pillow and escorted to a bed, surrounded by strangers I was now supposed to live with.

That night as I lay in bed, I heard a woman near me start to weep. I wondered if I should say something or just pretend I did not hear. But the crying continued. "Excuse me," I finally said, "is there something I can do for you?"

The crying stopped for a moment, then she replied, "No, I'm O.K." I didn't persist, since I felt there was little I could say to comfort her. After all, I was living in a shelter, too.

Before I fell asleep, I heard the faint whisper of a child in another part of the room. "Mom, when can we go home?" he whined. "Sh-sh, go to sleep now. We'll talk in the morning," the mother replied. I sobbed silently as I drifted off to sleep. I knew how that mother felt. What do you say to a child who has no home?

AFRAID TO REACH OUT

I spent the next morning looking for a job, but returned without any success. After lunch, I stood in a long line waiting to use the shelter's pay phone. The man on the line was begging someone to let his family stay with them for awhile. "Please. It won't be for long," he pleaded. "Just till I can get on my feet." When he hung up, I could tell by the look on his face that he'd been turned down.

The next caller, a woman, did no better. "They're putting us out tomorrow," she cried, "and I have nowhere else to go. Please, just for a day or two." I could see the fear in her eyes as she hung up.

At last it was my turn, and my heart beat wildly. I decided to call my sister one more time. When I picked up the phone, my hands were shaking so badly that I couldn't even dial. My sister had already made it quite clear she did not want me around; she was worried that her neighbors would find out I was homeless. So I set the phone down and went outside to cry.

That night I prayed silently that God would help me to escape poverty. God must have heard me, for I slept well for the first time in months.

FINDING WORK AND STARTING TO RECOVER

I spent the whole next day hunting for a job, and finally found one that afternoon at a fast-food restaurant. I was thrilled when the manager said I could start the next day. I knew that working for minimum wage would never get me out of poverty, but it was better than nothing. I got back to the shelter just in time for dinner. Bean soup and cornbread never tasted better.

That night, I noticed that the woman who had been crying the first night was gone. So was the mother whose child wondered why they couldn't go home. What had happened to them? Were they sleeping under a bridge or in an abandoned building? As I thanked God that night for helping me to find work, I prayed that each of them had found a home.

After many struggles and much hardship, my children and I now have a place to live. Although we are very far from being well off, we have managed to buy a home (with the help of Habitat for Humanity) and have started to gain back some of what we had lost to poverty. But it has taken years for us to feel secure enough to start living once again. I still wake up some nights, terrified that we might end up on the streets again.

GOD WILL SOMEDAY END POVERTY

Could it be that God is testing the hearts of us all by watching the way we treat the poor? What better way to try the heart and see if love or hate comes pouring forth? If we can sit by and watch as programs that feed and house the poor are cut, if we can pass by the homeless and forget the cries of the needy, then our own hearts condemn us.

In Proverbs, it says "Those who oppress the poor reproach their maker, but those who are kind to the needy honor God" (14:21). Those living in poverty are oppressed by businesses that pay low wages with no benefits. They are oppressed when they are forced to do work no one else wants, without being paid what they are worth. They are oppressed by people who believe they are less than human, just because they have no money.

Kindness to those in need honors God. It's so simple—maybe that's why it is overlooked. Proverbs 19:17 reads, "Whoever is kind to the poor lends to the Lord, and will be repaid in full." God must have great compassion for the suffering of those who are poor, if God would agree to cosign any loan to them!

The Scriptures assure us that God will remember the poor, even though they are forgotten by many others. The Bible testifies to God's great love and compassion for those who suffer, and declares that we will not always be oppressed, put down, and cast off. Let us join together in anticipation of that day when the bondage of poverty will be ripped away forever, and hunger will be no more.

Living in a Car

by Jackie Spinks

Jackie Spinks is a middle-aged white man who lives on the street. He has been without the financial means to afford a home for more than two decades. In the following narrative, Spinks describes his daily routine as a homeless person living out of a van in an unnamed American city.

Spinks's account reveals his resourcefulness, a skill picked up by nearly all homeless individuals. He details the ways in which he finds daily meals and gets an occasional shower, activities that average Americans take for granted. Throughout his narrative, Spinks offers some unique insights into the nature and experience of homelessness.

Spinks candidly discusses the state of his mental health. He claims to be regularly depressed and, as a result, to sleep a lot. He believes that his depression is related to the boredom of being out of work and lacking the stimuli enjoyed by people with money.

For seven months, my home has been my 1973 Dodge van. Life in a car is similar to life in a garbage can: trash filled, cramped, and with a smell to die from. Before that, I lived in a shed. I live here because I was kicked out of the shed.

Guys, suited in black worsted, the authority clothes of caliphs-in-waiting, circle around me; avoiding eye contact.

Sometimes I wonder what's going through their minds when they see me? Do they ever wonder what's going through mine? Or do they give a damn? Or maybe they assume I don't have a mind? Or are they thinking, "Bum! Loser! What's the matter with you? There's work out there. It isn't a recession. You corks think you're too good to work. So okay, be a stiff, but why do I have to support you, and why do you dirty up nice streets? Where's your pride? Where's your work ethic?"

Yeah, I pretty much know them. But they don't know me from marmalade. So here's to making my acquaintance.

LIVING AT THE BOTTOM

I'm one of those seedy guys at the bottom of American's class system, who knows that he's going to stay there. I'm not taken in by that "rags to riches" hooey our teachers, parents, media; in fact, the whole culture, fed us. I am 40-years-old, and have not earned more than $20,000 in my entire life, which means I've lived on less than $100 a month, for the past 20 years. So I know, after all this time, I'm not going anywhere.

Before I go on I'd better forewarn you: I'm not a curator of America's art of scrimping, a chronicler of poverty's abasements, or a bemoaner of its inequality. I'm just a down-and-outer trying to puzzle out my life, figure out how guys like me get where they are, especially when they don't have the excuse of alcohol or dope for their downward spiral.

AT HOME IN A VAN

I sold my Yamaha for $100 and bought this beater I'm living in for $75 dollars. Pretty lucky break. I got it for $75 because the interior was gutted, the windows broken, the roof rusted through. It was ready for the compactor, so nobody bid on it at the city auction. Thus, I have a home—my first in a long time.

I tinkered with it and got it moving. The reverse gear needs money to fix, so I can only go forward. The back brakes are bad (more money) and I worry driving, because of the brakes. So I don't drive it far. Besides, I have to hang onto my space, where my car's parked. But every once in a while I take a spin around the block just to keep my beater alive, as who knows when the local Praetorians will hustle me off. They'll give me a ticket for something, probably driving without registration. The constabulary knows and hates me. Not only am I an outcast, but being only five and a half feet tall, I'm an easy nab.

Mostly I stay where I am. What's important is keeping my corner. Three other guys have found my spot and are now parked near me. If I move my car, they'll grab it, as it is the best space, so I protect my claim. It's particularly valuable to me, as it's the only place where I can move forward and don't need to go into reverse.

It's a challenge, living in a crouched position in my van: minus toilet, water, telephone, electricity, and privacy. But the toughest part is the temperature: 95 degrees in the summer and freezing in winter.

GETTING FED AT THE MISSION

I eat at the mission. Before I forced myself to check out the place (I was afraid of it), I lived on stuff like vanilla wafers, nachos, half-eaten pizzas, or sandwiches I found lying around.

Why the mission spooked me was, first, it was strange; and second, a lot of beefy guys with nothing to lose hung around the entrance. I had no weapon, no back-up, and there's always some guy hankering to beat up a little guy. On the one hand, poverty makes brutes, but on the other hand, people are poor because they're basically passive. Telling myself they all just want to be somebody and have you recognize it, I stiffened my mettle.

Nevertheless, just to avoid trouble, I smiled. I'm the kind of guy who smiles a lot, tells jokes, shows he's a regular guy. But I confess the adrenaline was pumping, and a rigid smile was shellacked on my face when I ambled cool, but not cocky, into the mission. It smelled like fat frying, a good smell, and the eating space was big—a high-ceilinged room with about 80 guys and 2 women sitting at long tables. . . .

The food at the mission will never disturb McDonald's, but it fills me up and that's what counts. For instance, on my first day, they gave us two choices: bean soup or venison soup. We have a lot of deer hunters in this part of the country and most of them dislike venison, so the mission gets a lot of venison.

Most of the guys chose venison soup, but I chose bean soup. I'm a vegetarian, more by necessity than by conviction, but I think going without meat is a good idea. Besides, I have a soft spot for deer.

The mission, also, gets a lot of good pastries, the kind you buy at a bakery, usually about a week old. I eat a lot of doughnuts. You can take them with you when you leave. Sometimes we have ripe bananas. Sometimes we even have salad.

Often the food at the mission is spoiled, but nobody reports it, as it's better to be sick than risk closure. The bathroom, which is next to the kitchen, has been without toilet paper or paper towels for months. Four of the six toilets don't flush and nobody mops or uses cleanser, so you can figure it's a shopping mall of microbes, but nobody expects Trump Towers. Often I puke. Once, I did it for two days, but as one guy said, "How do you know it was the food at the mission. It could have been the flu."

Illness is for the rich. The poor that try to join that club, get two minutes and a swift heave-ho. It's been 20 years since I've been to a doctor. A few weeks back, I drove a guy with a severed finger to emergency, and sat with some mothers, who said they'd been waiting three hours. The mothers held their sick kids and scolded the others. . . .

My little forays into conversation with mission Saxons usually consist of mutual brag-a-thons. You'd think we'd all just dumped our portfolios with our brokers and decided to do a little slumming. And, if not that, we all have ships that will be tooting in, around the bend, any minute.

According to all of us displaced whites (I gas along with the best), we just need a little capital to get started. Some of the guys have pretty good ideas. One guy, a wood carver, thought he'd make Sasquash dolls and sell them at local fairs and bazaars. Another guy built a toilet for car dwellers, but fearing theft of his idea, was cagey in explaining how it operated. I listened up on that one. Then his paranoia took over, and he clammed up. Another had an idea for paper blankets.

It's all just talk. Nobody will ever do anything. To build up our self-esteem, we peg ourselves as 20th century pariahs, like frontier sheep farmers. We perceive ourselves as urban pioneers staking out claims, front runners of things to come. We carve out places, on the street, protect our turf, think of ourselves as prototypes of those guys who straggled over the Cascades without a penny to their names: sometimes desperate, often lonely, frequently surviving by their wits. They were giants. Stoics. Squatters like us. Our heroes. Deep in all of us, we mourn not having been born in the 18th century. Because we believe (probably incorrectly), that then poverty was a clean and honorable estate, not just wacko actions and fantasizing, like it is today.

THE DAY-TO-DAY ROUTINE OF HOMELESSNESS

How does a homeless, jobless, middle-aged man occupy his day? Well, first off, I sleep. Besides sleeping I post myself in the library. I arrive at opening time, ten in the morning, and stay most of the day. It's cool in there. Air conditioned. But temperature is only a minor reason I like the library. The main reason is the people. The people are quiet. No one bothers me or tells me to move on.

I read everything: religion, carpentry, mechanics, electrical, police training, political, biographies, nutrition, baseball novels, and a lot of gun, boat, news, and alternate press magazines. Sometimes I walk along the docks, examine the boats, imagine stowing away on a Russian cargo ship.

I scrutinize, with the eye of a tourist: buildings, factories, guys working—and I especially like to study bees. When I've exhausted looking, I sit in my car and read.

How do I live? Well, I use a can for my bowels and dump my loo near some pole beans and tomatoes in a garden nearby. I expected big beans and red, ripe tomatoes in that spot, but to my surprise they're limping along. One of my fellow car-dwelling aficionados said, "Living on the street, you probably got toxic crap." I do my "miss congeniality" smile, but don't think it's funny. I don't think he meant it to be funny. I use recycled newspaper for toilet paper.

I mosey up to the college about once a month and sneak a shower in the college gym. I'm careful to use it when it's empty, shower as quickly as possible, just in case I get caught.

Probably the biggest problem for guys like me is water. I'm always looking for water. Every chance I get, I fill up a jug I carry everywhere in my backpack and haul it back to my Dodge. And that's strictly for drinking—not to wash hands, face, dishes, or clothes.

DIRT IS EVIL

Apart from begging, the thing about poor people that riles rich people the most is our grime. Cleanliness is identified with goodness in America. It's next to Godliness. Dirt is evil. I think we're supposed to clean up and pretend we're real. I don't oppose cleanliness. It's that cleanliness for someone living in a car is a labyrinthine ordeal.

First, to wash and dry two loads of clothes—it costs about $5.00 total. Plus, you need a way to get to the laundry; plus, you need soap; plus, you need something to wear while you're washing the clothes.

But now and then a car-dwelling paisano does spiff up. Once cleaned up, he isn't too bad. I wonder why I've been going on ad nauseam about cleanliness and appearance? I must have some insecurity there. But then, so when aren't we insecure?

THOUGHTS ABOUT WORKING

As for work, in my 20s when hope bloomed, I choo-chooed along, the little engine that could—but not anymore. Now, it's "tote that barge, lift that bail, wish to hell I could land in jail." I've worked for bosses that were drill sergeants with little concern about their oxen's safety who expected it to plow away at minimum pay. I got chemical burns on my hands that ate away chunks of the flesh, burns that still eat my fingers ten years later. I have no hope for anything better than a grinding $4.60 an hour.

A guy at the mission said, "I'd rather be poor than work. Why should I help make the rich richer?"

I'm anxious all the time. Until I found the mission, I worried constantly about where my next meal was coming from; I was anxious about my future; anxious about people. But mostly I was anxious that if—by some remote possibility I landed a decent job—that after so many years of non-work, with its absence of punctuality, drive, and concentration, I would fail again.

Hey, I sound like the mother of all belly-achers, bitching about contaminated food, cleanliness, jobs, pisspots, anxiety. I forget the other class has troubles, too; that they whip themselves, unmercifully, if some friend gains on them. That if their cash flow falls from ten million to two million, they worry they're finished and stumble home, get swacked, and feel like they'll never be a real player.

I heard some social worker–type talk about homelessness being a new deviant career. Sure am glad I have a career at last. Deviant or otherwise. Is homelessness better than being male, white, 40, and working at McDonalds? Yeah, I guess so, but then, Hell, McDonalds wouldn't hire a bum like me—even if he did have nice teeth.

HOMELESSNESS AND MENTAL HEALTH

The inner awareness I live with, and fight every day is that I'm nothing. To get rid of this feeling, I'd like to try Prozac. But two bucks for a pill, without a buzz. Then again, maybe I'm lucky. At some later date, they'd probably discover Prozac caused some kink, like edema of the brain, or elephantiasis, or more likely, an old stand-by like high blood pressure or cancer. They always find some pea to stick in our comfort zone. So I sleep Prozacless.

Because I sleep a lot, the books I've read label me depressed. I question that, as I've never contemplated suicide; but maybe I am depressed and don't know it. Or maybe I sleep because I'm bored. About the only truism about poverty in America in the 1990s is that it's one giant yawn.

Maybe that's what depression is—nothing to do. Rutsville. And doing the rut alone, at ebb tide, and feeling it's all your fault. That everything's your fault. Feeling something's wrong with you because you would rather be poor than be under the foot of a master. So who wants to think. Better to sleep.

About our depression, whenever you channel onto a poor person's wave, male or female, what you discover is that—underneath the defenses—they're thinking, "There's something haywire with me. I'm worse than second-rate, I'm rotten. I can't do anything right. Nobody will ever hire a creep like me for any job that has a future. I'll never do anything that's even slightly smart."

To illustrate, a guy at the mission came out from lunch and found the side of his Kawasaki dented. A few minutes before he'd been chair of the brag-a-thon. Now, you'd expect the guy to say, "I'm gonna kill the bastard who did this." But no, all this poor jerk could do was stare and mutter, "It's all my fault. I can't do anything right."

We all walked away, but it hit close. We understood.

SOCIAL PERCEPTIONS OF THE HOMELESS

In contrast to Americans, who place so much emphasis on individualism, people from other countries don't blame themselves. A Hindu cab driver, so black that he felt forced to reiterate three times, to our un-inquiring minds, that he was Caucasian, told us about an experience he had here. He was sitting in a park and noticed several Americans going over to a marble protrusion, bending over it, and when water gushed out, drinking. Being thirsty, he went over to the protrusion, bent over it, but no water came out. He bent over it several times, still no water. Finally, he walked away, telling himself even the water over here in America is prejudiced.

Now that's what we considered an intelligent response, the kind we wish we could make.

It's like the world has a negative image of us, so we absorb that image, make it ours, and agree with the world, that, yes, because we aren't successes, we're slime.

SLOTH AND FREEDOM

Yeah, we're lazy. The dictionary definition of lazy is slow moving, resistant to exertion, slothful. And gadzooks, the perfect definition of depression.

Those active, employed people, who run around doing this and that, who talk briskly, walk with that high-stepping gait, who complain about having too much on their calendar, who, after a quick handshake, dash off to another appointment, are as strange to us as a bidet. We watch, wonder, and shuffle off, when we're around them. I guess they don't understand us either; the passive, the depressed, the underclass. Yet, we all share the same boat and it's gaining water. And maybe we know it better than they do.

Whatever. So, I sleep about 11 or 12 hours a day. Wish it were the sleep of the frazzled or anesthetized, but it's a half awake sleep. When awake I contemplate ways to make our world better. On good days, I dream of a revolution in concept. On bad days I decide, "Blow 'er up. Start over."

As I lie here, watching the rain drip alongside the car window, I forage around for something positive to say about poverty. What I come up with is freedom. Yeah, I have freedom—no worry about stocks or kids or lovers. I click around the idea of freedom for a while and finally decide, next to a high IQ, freedom is the most overrated quality any sociologist ever extolled.

Living on Welfare

Shoplifting the Necessities and More

by Rosa Lee Cunningham, with Leon Dash

In the early 1990s, Pulitzer Prize–winning author and former *Washington Post* reporter Leon Dash maintained close contact with a single-mother welfare recipient in order to write a book about her life and experiences. Rosa Lee Cunningham, an African American mother, grandmother, and heroin addict living in Maryland, was Dash's subject. In the following excerpt from his book, Dash concentrates on Rosa Lee's exploits as a shoplifter. While trying to remain neutral on the topic of theft, Dash allows Rosa Lee to explain why she steals. Rosa Lee attests that shoplifting has "helped her survive" when her welfare checks fail to cover the necessities. But as Dash notes, Rosa Lee steals more than just necessities and some of the profits from reselling the items go toward supporting her drug habit as well as her children's drug binges. Perhaps more troubling to Dash is the fact that Rosa Lee involves her own grandchildren in perpetrating the illegal acts. Rosa Lee, however, maintains that shoplifting is a skill that she is teaching them so that they will be able to get what they want in a world that seems to offer no escape from poverty.

Leon Dash is currently a professor of journalism at the University of Illinois at Urbana-Champaign.

R osa Lee guided her eleven-year-old grandson through the narrow aisles of a thrift shop in suburban Oxon Hill, Maryland, past the crowded racks of secondhand pants and shirts, stopping finally at the row of children's jackets and winter coats. Quickly, the boy selected a mock-leather flight jacket with a big number on the back and a price tag stapled to the collar.

"If you want it," Rosa Lee said, "then you're going to have to help me get it."

"Okay, Grandmama," he said nervously. "But do it in a way that I won't get caught."

Like a skilled teacher instructing a new student, Rosa Lee told her grandson what to do. "Pretend you're trying it on. Don't look up! Don't look around! Don't laugh like it's some kind of joke! Just put it on. Let Grandma see how you look."

The boy slipped off his old coat and put on the new one. Rosa Lee whispered, "Now put the other one back on, over it." She pushed down the new jacket's collar so that it was hidden.

"What do I do now?" he asked.

"Just walk on out the door," Rosa Lee said. "It's your coat." Four days later, Rosa Lee is recounting this episode for me, recreating the dialogue by changing her voice to distinguish between herself and her grandson. It is January 1991. By now, I have spent enough time with Rosa Lee that her shoplifting exploits no longer surprise me.

The previous November, Rosa Lee took her eight-year-old granddaughter into the same thrift shop on a Sunday morning to steal a new winter coat for the girl one week after they were both baptized in a Pentecostal church. On the Sunday of the shoplifting lesson, Rosa Lee had decided she did not want to take her granddaughter back to the church because her winter coat was "tacky and dirty."

In the thrift shop, Rosa Lee told her granddaughter to take off her coat and hang it on the coatrack. Next, she told the grinning child to put on the attractive pink winter coat hanging on the rack.

"Are we going to take this coat, Grandma?" asked the skinny little girl.

"Yes," Rosa Lee told her "We are exchanging coats. Now walk out the door."

STEALING TO SURVIVE

A month later, a week before Christmas, Rosa Lee was searching for something in a large shopping bag in her bedroom and dumped the contents onto the bed. Out spilled dozens of bottles of expensive men's cologne and women's perfume, as well as leather gloves with their sixty-dollar price tags still attached. She leaves the tags on when she sells the goods as proof of the merchandise's newness and quality.

"Did you get all this in one trip?" I ask.

"Oh, no," she says. "This is a couple of weeks' worth."

In Rosa Lee's younger years especially, shoplifting was a major source of income, supplementing her welfare payments and the money she made during fifteen years of waitressing at various nightclubs. With eight children to feed and clothe, stealing, she says, helped her survive. Later on, when she began using heroin in the mid-1970s, her shoplifting paid for drugs.

She stole from clothing stores, drugstores, and grocery stores, stuffing items inside the torn liner of her winter coat or slipping them into one of the oversized black purses that she carries wherever she goes. When her children were young—the ages of the grandson and granddaughter—she taught them how to shoplift as well.

"Every time I went somewhere to make some money, I would take my children," she said. "I would teach them or they would watch me. 'Just watch what Mama does. I'm getting food for y'all to eat.'"

In supermarkets, she could count on her children "to distract the security guard while I hit the meat freezer. The guards would always watch groups of children before they'd watch an adult."

Her favorite targets were the department stores. One of her two older brothers, Joe Louis Wright, joked with me one day that Rosa Lee "owned a piece" of Hecht's [department store] and had put Lansburgh's out of business. "Man, she would get coats, silk dresses," he recalled. "A cloth coat with a mink collar. She got me a mohair suit. Black. Three-piece. I don't know how the hell she'd get them out of there."

Her stealing has caused divisions and hard feelings in her family, and is one reason why Rosa Lee's relationships with several of her brothers and sisters are strained. They see Rosa Lee's stealing as an extreme and unjustified reaction to their impoverished upbringing. And her sons Alvin and Eric have always refused to participate in any of their mother's illegal activities.

UNDETERRED FROM SHOPLIFTING

Rosa Lee has served eight short prison terms for various kinds of stealing during the past forty years, dating back to the early 1950s. Her longest stay was eight months for trying to steal a fur coat from a Maryland department store in 1965. She says that she went to prison rehabilitation programs each time but that none had much of an effect on her. "I attended those programs so it would look good on my record when I went before the parole board," she says. "What they were talking about didn't mean anything to me. I didn't have the education they said would get me a job. I couldn't read no matter how many programs I went to."

Nothing seems to deter her from shoplifting, not even the specter of another jail term. On the day she directed her grandson in stealing the flight jacket, she was four days away from sentencing at the city's Superior Court for stealing the bedsheets from Hecht's the previous summer.

"I'm just trying to survive," she says.

STRETCHING THE TRUTH

Rosa Lee had chosen her clothes carefully for her appearance before Commissioner John Treanor in November. She wanted to look as poor as possible to draw his sympathy.

She wore an ill-fitting winter coat, gray wool overalls and a white wool hat pulled back to show her graying hair. She had removed her upper dental plate to give herself a toothless look when she smiled. "My homey look," she calls it. "No lipstick. No earrings. No nothing!"

Rosa Lee did not expect to go home that day. She saw a heavyset female deputy U. S. marshal move into place behind the defense table when the courtroom clerk called her name. It was a certain sign that Treanor had already decided to "step her back" and send her to jail. She hastily handed me her purse with all her documents.

"Hold on to these papers for me, Mr. Dash," she whispered. "Looks like I'm going to get some jail time. Tell my children where I'm at. You better come see me!"

Her lawyer's statements matched her downtrodden look. Rosa Lee's life was a mess, Elmer D. Ellis told Treanor. She was addicted to heroin, a habit she had developed in 1975. She was HIV positive. She was caring for three grandchildren because their mother was in jail.

Rosa Lee told Treanor that she was trying hard to turn herself around. She was taking methadone every day to control her heroin addiction and had turned again to the church. "I got baptized Sunday, me and my three grandchildren," she said, her voice breaking. "And I'm asking you from the bottom of my heart, give me a chance to prove that I'm taking my baptize seriously, 'cause I know I might not have much longer."

Tears ran down her cheeks. "I'm asking you for a chance, please," she begged Treanor. "I know I have a long record."

Rosa Lee was stretching the truth. Yes, she had been baptized, and yes, she was taking methadone. But no, she wasn't caring for her grandchildren alone. Their mother's jail term had ended in July, and she had returned to Rosa Lee's two-bedroom apartment to take care of the children, with help from Rosa Lee.

WAS I GOOD?

Treanor looked unimpressed with Rosa Lee's performance. He glowered at her, and Rosa Lee braced for the lecture she knew was coming. Both had played these roles before.

"Every time you pump yourself full of drugs and spend money to do it," he said, "you're stealing from your grandchildren. You're stealing food from their plates, clothes from their backs, and you're certainly jeopardizing their future. You're going to be one of the youngest dead grandmothers in town. And you're going to have three children that will be put up for adoption or going out to some home or some junior village or someplace."

That had been Rosa Lee's opening. "Can I prove to you that my life has changed?"

"Yeah, you can prove it to me, very simply," Treanor answered. "You can stay away from dope. Now I'll make a bargain with you. . . . You come back here the end of January and tell me what you've been doing, and then we'll think about it. But you're looking at jail time. You're looking at a cemetery."

Rosa Lee had won. Treanor postponed the sentencing. The marshal, who had moved in closer behind Rosa Lee at the start of Treanor's lecture, moved back. Treanor, red-faced with anger, called a ten-minute recess and hurriedly left the bench. Ellis shook Rosa Lee's hand.

Rosa Lee came over to me, her cheeks still tearstained but her face aglow. "Was I good?" she asked.

"Yeah," I said, startled at her boldness.

"Thank you," she said, smiling.

BACK AT IT

The marshal walked up to Rosa Lee. She too was smiling. She had escorted Rosa Lee and her daughters to the jail several times in the not-so-distant past. "You were going to jail, honey," she said to Rosa Lee. "You stopped him with those three grandchildren. He didn't want to have to deal with making arrangements for those children if he had sent you to jail. Is their mama still over [at] the jail?"

"Yes, she is," Rosa Lee lied, putting on a sad face. Five days before the hearing Rosa Lee was teaching her granddaughter how to shoplift. Through most of November and December, Rosa Lee stole cologne, perfume, gloves, and brightly colored silk scarves to sell to people who used them as Christmas presents. The day before her court appearance, she and a fellow drug-clinic patient, Jackie, were shoplifting in a drugstore one block from the Superior Court building shortly after they had drunk their morning meth [methadone].

A Teen Grows Up Fast

by Neesa Ray

In the following article with *Teen Magazine*'s Stephanie Booth, Neesa Ray, a teenage girl, talks about her and her family's life in poverty. Neesa says that her father was wrongfully accused of a crime and arrested when she was twelve years old. In order to come up with the money for a trial lawyer, Neesa's family sold most of their belongings. When the lawyer left town with the money, the Ray family sank into financial ruin. The family qualified for welfare, but they received less than enough money to cover their basic needs.

Neesa describes the restructuring her family had to go through in the absence of both a father figure and a steady income. She also discusses the effects that poverty had on her personal life. Being a teen and not having money, Neesa claims, is a tough way to grow up. She cites several instances of awkwardness and embarrassment at being surrounded by friends who were part of financially stable households. Her poverty, she says, affected everything from what food she ate to her social life.

At the close of her narrative, sixteen-year-old Neesa expresses that growing up in poverty was difficult for her as a youngster but now that she is older, she appreciates the lessons she learned. Living through poverty made her mature faster than many of her peers, and she discovered the value of being responsible with her time and money.

When I was 12, my life was probably a lot like yours. My family was living in southern Florida—OK neighborhood, OK house. My dad was working as an electrician and my mom looked after us kids—me and my two little sisters, Triva and Lynne—while pregnant with my third sister, Luanna. We didn't have a ton of money, but if I needed something, my parents would buy it for me.

Then everything changed.

One morning, the police burst into our house and arrested my dad, claiming he was a fugitive and had assaulted a woman in New

Jersey two months before. None of us believed it was true, and we stood behind Dad—but the price was steep. First, we gave up everything—our house, our car, our furniture—to hire a criminal lawyer. Almost my whole world was sold at a garage sale over one weekend to help pay for the $25,000 attorney's fee.

After we sold all our stuff, we moved up to Trenton, N.J., where my dad was in jail. When we arrived, mom got us a room in a cheap motel on the highway. The place was dark and dingy, and it gave me the creeps. It wasn't safe either. People were dealing drugs in plain view, there were screaming fights—one night, someone got shot. My sisters were too young to understand what was going on, but I was terrified.

Things got even worse when the lawyer we hired ran off with our money. We had no way of finding him, and nothing left to help my dad. The court assigned him some public defender who didn't seem to care about any of us—and she lost the case. At the very same moment I was at the hospital watching my mom give birth to my third sister, my dad was being sentenced to eight years in state prison.

ON THE SKIDS

"We're only going to be here a little while," my mom promised when we first got to the motel, but that "little while" turned into three and a half years. While she was out looking for work or visiting my dad, I stayed "home" and watched my sisters. I took care of my new sister so much that it was like I had a real-life baby of my own and I was only 12.

We got on welfare, but we only qualified for $382 a month, plus $400 in food stamps. That wasn't even enough for the basics and almost nothing for clothes or school supplies. We made the money stretch by cutting coupons from newspapers people left at the laundromat and collecting cans and bottles for a few extra dollars. We stopped buying brand name groceries and only got soda if it was someone's birthday.

School was my great escape. At school, I didn't have to think about the depressing motel, change diapers or hear my sisters bickering. One day, I was sick with a 103-degree temperature and I still went to school for peace and quiet. I just laid down in the nurse's office all day.

I made some friends, but none of them knew about my dad or how bad off we were. I said I lived a couple of miles away and my mom always dropped me off at the bus stop because it was on her way to work. That was the biggest lie I told. Most of the time I tried not to say anything.

Like with lunches. I never brought my lunch because I didn't want anyone to see there was no meat in my sandwiches, or that we had to use toilet paper for napkins. By lunch time, though, I was so hungry that I got to eating other people's food. They'd have unfinished roast beef sandwiches or bags of chips they were too full to eat, and I'd take them. I wouldn't act ashamed or anything, I'd just make a big joke out of it so everyone else did too. They thought I had this really big appetite.

I missed having friends come over after school, but what would we do at the motel? We didn't have a TV. I didn't have video games or CDs, much less anything to play them on. Sharing a bed with my mom and my sisters didn't bother me, but I didn't want people to feel sorry for me.

I also missed going out. When girls asked me to go to the movies, I could never go. I'd make up excuses or say I had to baby-sit. I didn't see a movie for all those years! Once, I talked my mom into letting me take the bus to the mall to meet my friend Nicole. Going shopping with her was weird because Nicole's mom just handed over the charge card. That Saturday, she bought a $12 bottle of shampoo and some glittery gold lipstick I knew she'd never wear. Her grandma also gave her a $60 gift certificate, and she spent it all on one shirt. I couldn't believe it! I kept thinking, "One shirt! I could have bought six things with that much money!" I just pretended there was nothing I liked.

Dating was really hard, too, since I didn't have time to hang out after school and meet boys. Once there was a big dance and this guy, Rex, asked me to go. I was excited about being asked out, but I knew I couldn't go. I told him no in a kind of mean way, and walked off. Later, Nicole told me Rex thought I was stuck up and cold—he didn't understand. See, whenever there was something I really wanted to do—like go to a dance or a birthday party—money always got in the way. I couldn't afford a dress or a gift.

After I turned Rex down, Nicole went off on me. She started yelling, saying my mom took advantage of me, and that I needed to get a life. She even said something to one of our teachers, who turned around and called up my mom. My mom didn't tell her about my dad, or how we lived. She just said, "Neesa doesn't need a life at school. Her life's here with her family."

REAL VALUES ARE PRICELESS

Sometimes I wish I were rich like Nicole and could go out to dinner with my parents, or get my nails done just because I feel like it. But I try to deal. I know I'm more mature than other girls my age because I've had to grow up fast. I'm smart with money and better with kids than a lot of adults I know.

I'm 16 now. When I think of where I'm at and where I want to be, sometimes I do get a little down. But things are improving. We're out of the motel now and living in a real house, but my dad's still in prison and won't be up for parole for another three years. I'm still the one who takes care of my sisters while my mom works at the dry cleaners down the street.

Whenever I get depressed, or start wishing I had the nice things other girls my age do, I look at how much I help my mom and how well my sisters are growing up, and I feel proud. When I talk to my dad he tells me how much he counts on me and how proud he is too. That means more to me than money ever could.

The Plight of the Rural Poor

by Nick Middleton

Nick Middleton is a fellow in physical geography at St. Anne's College, Oxford. He is also a freelance author who has written more than two hundred articles and sixteen books. In 1999 Middleton embarked on a journey through America's Deep South along Highway 61 as part of his research for a travel narrative. In the following article, which covers part of that trek, Middleton describes the flat, agricultural landscape and the dire poverty that, to him, seem to characterize the Mississippi Delta region. As Middleton notes, the majority of towns in the delta are home to an overwhelming number of poor African Americans, since the whites who could afford to move left the agricultural belt long ago. The few well-to-do whites who remained now reside on big corporate farms, while the destitute, disproportionately black populations—the remnants of failed sharecropping ventures that date back to the post–Civil War years—languish in joblessness and a reliance on government aid. Although most of the poor living in the Deep South seem unable to break the cycle of poverty, one new industry is offering some hope. Several southern states have legalized casinos as a means of increasing revenues, and as Middleton explains, the poor are availing themselves of whatever menial work is available in these new multimillion-dollar enterprises. Although the long-term economic impact of casinos may be controversial, Middleton asserts that at least the job opportunities offer a few lucky souls a potential ticket out of the poverty that has gripped the region for so long.

It was January, a wet and miserable morning as I drove south out of Memphis, on to Highway 61 and into the Mississippi Delta. The first feeling that hit me was a sense of the infinite. The agricultural landscape was gigantic and relentlessly flat. The fields I passed

Nick Middleton, "Mississippi Blues," *Geographical*, vol. 71, July 1999. Copyright © 1999 by Savedash Ltd (UK). Reproduced by permission.

were the size of small counties and the countryside was so level that most of the scenery was sky.

Highway 61 is known as the "Main Street" of the Mississippi Delta, the rich alluvial bottomlands that stretch between the Mississippi and Yazoo rivers. This is the heart of the US Deep South, the spiritual home of [author] William Faulkner and [playwright] Tennessee Williams, a mythical land of antebellum mansions and sprawling plantations, of syrupy accents and Spanish moss streamers.

The Deep South is roughly coincident with the old Cotton Belt, where nature supplies more than 200 frost-free days every year along with at least 110 centimetres of rain. Before cotton became king, the Mississippi Delta was a primeval wilderness of forest and wetland, but the trees were felled and the swamps drained to make way for the crop that made the South's fortune.

The scenery had little colour beyond the dark earth and a few surviving dun-coloured trees. When I passed a place selling John Deere tractors, the virulent green of the machines seemed like the visual equivalent of shouting in church. The weather didn't help. If I'd come in the summer, no doubt all would have been tractor green—not with cotton nowadays, more likely with soya. But in early January the centre-pivot irrigation booms just stood motionless beside the road like huge, grubby insects and the sun was nowhere to be seen. The panorama was vast, drab and dreary.

POVERTY OF THE DEEP SOUTH

Although much of the cotton has gone, you can still delineate the Deep South by locating rural communities with populations more than 25 per cent black. Alabama, Georgia, Louisiana and South Carolina are all Deep South states, but Mississippi is supposed to be the deepest and most southern of them all. It's the South's South. They say that if Mississippi was any more Southern, it would be a foreign country. When, some years back, [social welfare activist, the Reverend] Jesse Jackson came to this part of the world, he thought it was: he called it "America's Ethiopia."

I got an idea of what Mr Jackson was talking about as I drove on down into the Delta and saw the poverty. Not charming, honest, rural poverty, but the grimy, squalid, no-hope variety you normally associate with urban ghettos. It came in a string of settlements with bright and breezy names that mocked their true status: places like Rich, Bobo, Hushpuckena and Merigold.

The length of Highway 61 was littered with these depressing apologies for towns hemmed in by deep storm ditches full of crud and garbage. Gruesome shacks with mud drives punctuated derelict shopfronts and abandoned filling stations. The farther I drove into the heart of the Delta, the worse the road became. It was possible to drive at 55 miles-per-hour, like the signs said I could, but the regular potholes made the going decidedly uncomfortable. At Bobo, most of the dilapidated houses sat very close to waterlogged terrain, indicating the importance of minor variations in elevation in such a level land.

On the outskirts of Mound Bayou, people appeared to be living in an old school bus. In town, the smartest building by a long way was the African Methodist Episcopal church. A large hoarding [billboard] declared the settlement to be the oldest all-black municipality in the USA. It was settled on July 12, 1887 by former slaves of one Jo Davis, who conceived the idea before the Civil War, or "the War Between the States", as many Southerners still like to call it. The notice stood in front of a hospital that had long ceased to function. On the other side of the road, a former gas station looked like it hadn't served fuel since the prohibition era.

CRUMBLING COMMUNITIES

There isn't much call for fuel in Mound Bayou because nearly half the households don't own a motor vehicle. I was surprised to see a couple of operational gas stations in Shelby, where nearly three-quarters of black households don't have a car. These proportions are rather higher than the national average: in the US as a whole, just eight percent of households are non vehicle-owners. But these are the sort of statistics that the Mississippi Delta is renowned for. Winstonville, another all-black town like Mound Bayou, has 66 per cent of its population living below the poverty line. This is why this sorry string of spiritless communities looks like the remnants of some terrible holocaust. They are places where the only pleasant buildings are the churches, and virtually the only other properties that aren't slowly mouldering are the occasional banks which exist solely because of the infusion of social security payments.

With an irony that somehow typifies the South, they have reached this state partly in response to the success of the civil rights movement of the 1950s and 60s. Ever since the schools became integrated, the Mississippi Delta's whites have been moving out, taking their wealth with them and leaving the poorer blacks behind. Historically, Mound Bayou and Winstonville have always been all-black towns, but others have been getting steadily blacker, and steadily poorer, over the past few decades. In 1950, 55 per cent of Alligator's 200-odd residents were black. By 1990, they comprised 75 per cent. In Shelby, the percentage was 62 in 1950, but it passed the 80 per cent mark 40 years later. The same pattern has been repeated all over the Delta.

CHANGES IN THE AGRICULTURAL ECONOMY

The roots of the poverty are buried in the cycle of Delta land use since its initial clearance for agriculture. King Cotton and his plantations had taken over the Mississippi Delta's fertile soils by the eve of the War Between the States. Emancipation of the slaves didn't do much to alter the agricultural nature of the area. Instead of working the plantations in slave gangs, the Delta's blacks became sharecroppers working their individual plots (although most of the land was still owned by the planters). Slowly, sharecroppers moved away from their nucleated quarters by the planters' mansions and took up residence in cabins built on the plots that they worked. During the 1930s, a period of dramatic change began in the rural South. Farms and plantations started to become mechanised and reorganised, and so began a mass black exodus from the land. The introduction of tractors in the 1930s was followed by mechanical cotton harvesters in the late 1940s and by the increasing use of herbicides in the 1950s. Sharecroppers abandoned their cabins and moved into town or out of the South altogether, to the cities of the US north and west. The agricultural landscape had come full circle and huge neo-plantations, hauntingly reminiscent of their antebellum counterparts, had become the order of the day.

A similar process has been repeated across the rural South. In 1940, more than seven in ten rural Southern blacks lived on farms. By 1980, the figure had fallen below three in a hundred. But nowhere have the results been more pronounced than on the Mississippi Delta because Mississippi is the South's South and the Delta is Mississippi's Mississippi. For the sharecroppers that ended up in places like Shelby, Alligator and Mound Bayou, there was little in the way of alternative employment. It was a straight swap: sharecropping for a welfare cheque. Some see their plight in similar terms to the cycle that saw the pre-war plantations eventually transformed into neo-plantations. From slavery, the Southern black had tasted independence as a sharecropper and then been thrust back to rely on federal patronage. Many of those with jobs in the Delta ghetto towns are simply employed in administering the dependency of their communities on social security payments. Academics have devised a term for it: welfare colonialism.

When politicians talk of alleviating poverty and creating jobs they usually concentrate on the urban poor. The rural poor stuck in the welfare trap continue to suffer because they aren't even on the public's radar screen. They are as likely to find work by scanning the "help wanted" ads as the obituaries. They can't even enjoy the sorts of benefits you might think were some compensation for being the rural poor—the countryside isn't pleasant and pretty, it's just an endless expanse of corporate fields.

CASINO OPPORTUNITIES

One way out of this economic backwater lay back up Highway 61 in Tunica County. In the early 1990s this was the setting for an exercise in the bizarre that could only happen in the USA. They started building casinos. The hoardings leading you towards them had started to appear on the outskirts of Memphis like lights on the road to Damascus: "Jumbo-size casino thrills", "Vegas-style action in a spectacular river setting". It was Disneyland in Ethiopia.

I spent a couple of nights at Fitzgeralds, a casino and hotel inside a huge mock castle that rose out of the Mississippi floodplain like Camelot in a kingdom of mud. The place was surreal. If I had arrived during the 100-degree summer, I'd have thought it was a mirage. Fitzgeralds was like Xanadu in the netherworld. It was Faulkner's Yoknapatawpha County on crack-cocaine.

DIXIELAND'S VEGAS

Morning, noon and night were all the same in the cavernous gaming halls because they have no windows. Twenty-four hours a day punters [gamblers] wandered back and forth, transfixed by the flashing lights, carrying large plastic cups full of quarters to feed the slot machines. Mississippi reckons on using the huge revenues from its Dixie Vegas for the state's education system, but critics of the casino approach to economic development point to the fragility of the get-rich-quick mentality and the fact that casinos don't actually tend to boost local economies. Gamblers rarely leave the grounds of the casinos, their hotels and restaurants undercut any facilities, and many of the punters are locals who can't really afford to gamble.

But the casinos do provide some jobs for local communities. I knew this because all of the staff had been issued with name badges that also gave the name of their home towns. Among the waitresses I noticed Sharlene from Clarksdale, Melody from Batesville, Yoland from Tunica, and Lawanda from Hernando. Melody from Batesville brought me a beer in the sports bar one evening and she paused to chat for a while. She worked the evening shift, she told me, 6 pm to 2 am, and it took her another hour to drive home afterwards. "It must be tiring," I said. "Yeah, but the money's right," Melody replied. We were interrupted by a shout from the casino. "He's here," cried a man jubilantly. "It's Elvis. Elvis is in the house." And everybody cheered. Like most Elvis lookalikes, this guy was impersonating the later, mutton-chop sideburn version of the King. He looked the part in a white mirror-studded jump suit complete with rhinestones and a red eagle on the back. Up front, the jump-suit was open all the way down to its huge belt buckle.

Elvis Presley was born and raised just up the road in the small town of Tupelo. A true product of the Delta, he absorbed the black chants in the cotton fields, the gospel music in the pews of the Assembly of God, and the Mississippi blues that were all around him. He put them all together and became a rock and roll legend. It was his ticket out of the dark tunnel of poverty that was, and still is, the Mississippi Delta.

CHAPTER 3

The Working Poor

The Harsh Realities of Low-Wage Labor

by Barbara Ehrenreich

In the following article, social and political commentator Barbara Ehrenreich describes her experience of working for a maid service and bearing witness to the lives of her coworkers, many of whom are among the working poor. Ehrenreich details the contrast in lifestyles between her fellow maids, who find it hard to come up with the money for a meager lunch, and the people whose houses they clean, people who can afford to hire an army of maids to neaten their massive homes. She makes the claim that choosing to work as a maid in the first place is a good indicator of how destitute many of her coworkers are. The reality of the working poor becomes apparent to Ehrenreich as, among other things, she watches her fellow maids save half-smoked cigarettes and listens to them talk about how to get free health care. The significance of the situation for her, however, lies in the fact that the people she works with are forgoing basic human needs such as food and water during their workday to tend to the needs of people who have an excess of comfort.

Barbara Ehrenreich is a writer and activist whose articles have appeared in such publications as *Mother Jones*, *Harper's*, and *Time*. She has also written twelve books on a variety of topics.

Liza, a good-natured woman in her thirties who is my first team leader, explains that we are given only so many minutes per house, ranging from under sixty for a 1-½-bathroom apartment to two hundred or more for a multi-bathroom "first timer." I'd like to know why anybody worries about [the official] time limits if we're being paid by the hour but hesitate to display anything that might be interpreted as attitude. As we get to each house, Liza assigns our tasks, and I cross my fingers to ward off bathrooms and vacuuming. Even dusting, though, gets aerobic under pressure, and after about

Barbara Ehrenreich, *Nickel and Dimed: On (Not) Getting by in America.* New York: Metropolitan, 2001. Copyright © 2001 by Barbara Ehrenreich. All rights reserved. Reproduced by permission of Henry Holt and Company, LLC.

an hour of it—reaching to get door tops, crawling along floors to wipe baseboards, standing on my bucket to attack the higher shelves—I wouldn't mind sitting down with a tall glass of water. But as soon as you complete your assigned task, you report to the team leader to be assigned to help someone else. Once or twice, when the normal process of evaporation is deemed too slow, I am assigned to dry a scrubbed floor by putting rags under my feet and skating around on it. Usually, by the time I get out to the car and am dumping the dirty water used on floors and wringing out rags, the rest of the team is already in the car with the motor running. Liza assures me that they've never left anyone behind at a house, not even, presumably, a very new person whom nobody knows.

WORKING POOR

In my interview, I had been promised a thirty-minute lunch break, but this turns out to be a five-minute pit stop at a convenience store, if that. I bring my own sandwich—the same turkey breast and cheese every day—as do a couple of the others; the rest eat convenience store fare, a bagel or doughnut salvaged from our free breakfast, or nothing at all. The two older married women I'm teamed up with eat best—sandwiches and fruit. Among the younger women, lunch consists of a slice of pizza, a "pizza pocket" (a roll of dough surrounding some pizza sauce), or a small bag of chips. Bear in mind we are not office workers, sitting around idling at the basal metabolic rate. A poster on the wall in the office cheerily displays the number of calories burned per minute at our various tasks, ranging from about 3.5 for dusting to 7 for vacuuming. If you assume an average of 5 calories per minute in a seven-hour day (eight hours minus time for travel between houses), you need to be taking in 2,100 calories in addition to the resting minimum of, say, 900 or so. I get pushy with Rosalie, who is new like me and fresh from high school in a rural northern part of the state, about the meagerness of her lunches, which consist solely of Doritos—a half bag from the day before or a freshly purchased small-sized bag. She just didn't have anything in the house, she says (though she lives with her boyfriend and his mother), and she certainly doesn't have any money to buy lunch, as I find out when I offer to fetch her a soda from a Quik Mart and she has to admit she doesn't have eighty-nine cents. I treat her to the soda, wishing I could force her, mommylike, to take milk instead. So how does she hold up for an eight—or even nine-hour day? "Well," she concedes, "I get dizzy sometimes."

How poor are they, my coworkers? The fact that anyone is working this job at all can be taken as prima facie evidence of some kind of desperation or at least a history of mistakes and disappointments, but it's not for me to ask. In the prison movies that provide me with a mental guide to comportment, the new guy doesn't go around shaking hands and asking, "Hi there, what are you in for?" So I listen, in the cars and when we're assembled in the office, and learn, first, that no one seems to be homeless. Almost everyone is embedded in extended families or families artificially extended with housemates. People talk about visiting grandparents in the hospital or sending birthday cards to a niece's husband; single mothers live with their own mothers or share apartments with a coworker or boyfriend. Pauline, the oldest of us, owns her own home, but she sleeps on the living room sofa, while her four grown children and three grandchildren fill up the bedrooms.

But although no one, apparently, is sleeping in a car, there are signs, even at the beginning, of real difficulty if not actual misery. Half-smoked cigarettes are returned to the pack. There are discussions about who will come up with fifty cents for a toll and whether Ted [their office-bound supervisor] can be counted on for prompt reimbursement. One of my teammates gets frantic about a painfully impacted wisdom tooth and keeps making calls from our houses to try to locate a source of free dental care. When my—or, I should say, Liza's—team discovers there is not a single Dobie in our buckets, I suggest that we stop at a convenience store and buy one rather than drive all the way back to the office. But it turns out I haven't brought any money with me and we cannot put together $2 among the four of us.

ON THE JOB

The Friday of my first week at The Maids is unnaturally hot for Maine in early September—95 degrees, according to the digital time-and-temperature displays offered by banks that we pass. I'm teamed up with the sad-faced Rosalie and our leader, Maddy, whose sullenness, under the circumstances, is almost a relief after Liza's relentless good cheer. Liza, I've learned, is the highest-ranking cleaner, a sort of supervisor really, and said to be something of a snitch, but Maddy, a single mom of maybe twenty-seven or so, has worked for only three months and broods about her child care problems. Her boyfriend's sister, she tells me on the drive to our first house, watches her eighteen-month-old for $50 a week, which is a stretch on The Maids' pay, plus she doesn't entirely trust the sister, but a real day care center could be as much as $90 a week. After polishing off the first house, no problem, we grab "lunch"—Doritos for Rosalie and a bag of Pepperidge Farm Goldfish for Maddy—and head out into the exurbs for what our instruction sheet warns is a five-bathroom spread and a first-timer to boot. Still, the size of the place makes us pause for a moment, buckets in hand, before searching out an appropriately humble entrance. It sits there like a beached ocean liner, the prow cutting through swells of green turf, windows without number. "Well, well," Maddy says, reading the owner's name from our instruction sheet, "Mrs. W. and her big-ass house. I hope she's going to give us lunch."

Mrs. W. is not in fact happy to see us, grimacing with exasperation when the black nanny ushers us into the family room or sunroom or den or whatever kind of specialized space she is sitting in. After all, she already has the nanny, a cook-like person, and a crew of men doing some sort of finishing touches on the construction to supervise. No, she doesn't want to take us around the house, because she already explained everything to the office on the phone, but Maddy stands there, with Rosalie and me behind her, until she relents. We are to move everything on all surfaces, she instructs during the tour, and get underneath and be sure to do every bit of the several miles, I calculate, of baseboards. And be mindful of the baby, who's napping and can't have cleaning fluids of any kind near her.

HEAT AND DUST

Then I am let loose to dust. In a situation like this, where I don't even know how to name the various kinds of rooms, The Maids' special system turns out to be a lifesaver. All I have to do is keep moving from left to right, within rooms and between rooms, trying to identify landmarks so I don't accidentally do a room or a hallway twice. Dusters get the most complete biographical overview, due to the necessity of lifting each object and tchotchke individually, and I learn that Mrs. W. is an alumna of an important women's college, now occupying herself by monitoring her investments and the baby's bowel movements. I find special charts for this latter purpose, with spaces for time of day, most recent fluid intake, consistency, and color. In the master bedroom, I dust a whole shelf of books on pregnancy, breastfeeding, the first six months, the first year, the first two years—and I wonder what the child care-deprived Maddy makes of all this. Maybe there's been some secret division of the world's women into breeders and drones, and those at the maid level are no longer supposed to be reproducing at all. Maybe this is why our office manager, Tammy, who was once a maid herself, wears inch-long fake nails and tarty little outfits—to show she's advanced to the breeder caste and can't be sent out to clean anymore.

It is hotter inside than out, un-air-conditioned for the benefit of the baby, I suppose, but I do all right until I encounter the banks of glass doors that line the side and back of the ground floor. Each one has to be Windexed, wiped, and buffed—inside and out, top to bottom, left to right, until it's as streakless and invisible as a material substance can be. Outside, I can see the construction guys knocking back Gatorade, but the rule is that no fluid or food item can touch a maid's lips when she's inside a house. Now, sweat, even in unseemly quantities, is nothing new to me. I live in a subtropical area where even the inactive can expect to be moist nine months out of the year. I work out, too, in my normal life and take a certain macho pride in the Vs of sweat that form on my T-shirt after ten minutes or more on the StairMaster. But in normal life, fluids lost are immediately replaced. Everyone in yuppie-land—airports, for example—looks like a nursing baby these days, inseparable from their plastic bottles of water. Here, however, I sweat without replacement or pause, not in individual drops but in continuous sheets of fluid soaking through my polo shirt, pouring down the backs of my legs. The eyeliner I put on in the morning—vain twit that I am—has long since streaked down onto my cheeks, and I could wring my braid out if I wanted to. Working my way through the living room(s), I wonder if Mrs. W. will ever have occasion to realize that every single doodad and objet through which she expresses her unique, individual self is, from another vantage point, only an obstacle between some thirsty person and a glass of water.

Providing for a Family of Eight on a Limited Income

by Mark and Linda Armstrong,
interviewed by Steven VanderStaay

The Armstrongs are an African American family of eight (two parents and six children) who once lived in the affluent city of Bellevue, Washington. They were doing well for themselves financially when Mark, the head of the household, lost his job and had to pay for emergency surgery for one of their sons. The family could no longer afford their home and were forced to move to nearby Seattle. Now Mark and his wife, Linda, as well as the older children, must make the commute back to Bellevue in order to get to their lower-paying jobs.

In the following interview with Steven VanderStaay, Mark and Linda discuss the struggles of maintaining a family on less-than-adequate monetary means.

Steven VanderStaay is an associate professor of English at Western Washington University. He has written many articles for various publications and has penned a book called *Street Lives: An Oral History of Homeless Americans*, from which this excerpt was taken.

Mark: I designed and built conveyor belts, and was good at it. I was making over $15 an hour. And I can go back there right now and get you a letter of recommendation from the company and let you read what they wrote about me. That in itself tells you what kind of worker I am.

MINIMUM WAGE IS INSULTING

The company went out of business. Bang! Didn't even know it was coming. I was between jobs three or four months. I could have found work right away if I wanted to make minimum wage, but I got pretty high standards for myself. I don't even want to make what I'm

Steven VanderStaay, *Street Lives: An Oral History of Homeless Americans*. Philadelphia, PA: New Society, 1992. Copyright © 1992 by Steven VanderStaay. Reproduced by permission of the author.

making now. We could barely afford rent then, how can we now? But when you got kids to feed and bills to pay, you have to do the best you can.

But minimum wage—that's insulting. I don't knock it for high school students. They're getting training, learning about working, making their pocket money. That's fine. But you take a person . . . I got six kids. $3.35, $4 an hour, I spend more than that wage in a day's time on a grocery bill. I mean you can accept some setbacks, but you can't tell a person, "I don't care if you've been making $15 something an hour, the minimum is what you've got to make now." If I hand you this letter, give you my resumé, my military record, show you the kind of worker I am, talk about my family, how can you degrade me by offering me the minimum wage?

Then we had trouble with the house we were renting. And, well, the biggest part of it was hospital bills. My son had to have emergency surgery. Since the company was going out of business it let the insurance lapse, so I got stuck with the bill. Spent every penny we had saved and there's still fourteen hundred dollars on it. You would think by being medical that it wouldn't affect the credit, but it does.

Now I'm working with Safeway's warehouse. I work in the milk plant. Swing shift. Sometimes I'm off at 12:30, 1:00 at night, and then turn right around and go back at 8:30 the next morning. Yeah, it's hard sometimes, I'm not making half of what I used to. I'm a helper—I used to have people working for me. I'd worked my way up through the ranks. But like I was saying, you adjust, you do what you have to do. I'm the kind of person, I get with a company I want to stay, be a part of it. I like to get along with people and work, get my hands dirty. See something accomplished. I'm low man on the totem pole but I'll stay and work my way up. . . .

WORK, SCHOOL, AND FAMILY

Linda: I've been a custodian, nurse's aid; now I work at K-Mart. I still have to bus back to the East side [Bellevue] every day. It's okay but I'm looking for something else. You know, it's $4 an hour, and there's no benefits, no discounts at the store, nothing like that.

And I'm in school now, too. I'm going for business training, probably computers or administration. When school starts I'll either bring the little ones there with me or have one of the older ones bring them home.

Working full-time and going to school. Six kids, seventeen on down to twelve. Three in high school, three in grade school. Two of them work at Jack in the Box. They've been working the same shift but my oldest, he's on the football team, so he might be working at a different time than my daughter. And then there's the church, and those football games. Yes we're busy! Just an all-American family. One that's hit a string of bad luck, that's all.

The hardest thing is getting up early enough to bus back over there. As soon as school gets started that's really going to be a problem. It might be a couple of hours, both ways. And if they find out our kids are living here they'll want them in school in Seattle. But they like the schools there and I like them. They're better. And that's where we've lived, that's where we work.

But we get by. The kids, they cook, they clean, they wash and iron their own clothes. And the older ones, they all work. We're so proud of them. Oh, we have the same problems everybody else has, with teenagers and so forth. But we get through 'em. Just thank God they're not on drugs. That's the biggest problem here.

BEING STRAIGHT WITH THE KIDS

Mark: When we had to move and lost the house, when I lost my job, we told the kids the truth, the flat out truth. With no misconception; none whatsoever. Kids are not dumb. If you lie to kids, why should they be honest with you? They know exactly what we're going through and they know why.

Same thing when we moved here—six kids, three rooms, writing all over the walls, the drugs and crime. We tried to avoid the move but we didn't have any choice. They knew exactly where we were moving to, as best as I could explain it. We told them we didn't want to come, but if it came down to it we were coming. And we did.

Now my worst fear . . . there's so much drugs in this area. And people think every apartment in the projects is a drug house. They knock on the doors, knock on the windows—they stop me out there and ask where it is. It's here, so close to us all the times. And all the shooting and fighting . . . you can look out the window any given night and see the police stopping people and searching everyone.

If I can't look out my door and see my kids, I send for 'em. And I'm afraid when I can't see 'em. 'Cause when they get to shootin' and fightin' and carryin'-on a bullet don't got no names on it. Sometimes when I come in from work, three, four o'clock in the morning, I wonder just when they're going to get me. But my worst fear, my worst fear is the kids. . . .

TRYING TO RENT A HOME

People don't want to rent to a family. And you know the kind of rent they're asking over there in Bellevue, that's not easy to come up with. And you need first, last month's rent, security. . . . And then people automatically assess, they stereotype you. Maybe sometimes it's 'cause we're black—I'm not saying this is true, I'm saying that sometimes I *felt* that the reason we didn't get a place was because we were black. But most of the time it's the family. People would rather you have pets than kids these days.

One guy, he had six bedrooms in this house. But he didn't want a family. Why would you have six bedrooms if you didn't want to rent to a family? May not be legal, but they do that all the time.

Now there is some validity in what they say about children tearing up things. But the child is only as bad as you let him be. You're the parent, he's going to do exactly what you let him do and get away with. If my kids tear something up I'll pay for it. But me, I tell my kids that if I have to replace something they've destroyed, then one of their sisters or brothers isn't going to get something they need. And when they do something they answer to me.

NOT TREATED RIGHT

I'm not bitter . . . I mean I'm somewhat so. I'm not angry bitter. It's just that I don't like dragging my kids from one place to the next, and I don't think we've been treated right. We had to take places sight-unseen, just to get 'em. We paid $950 a month, and during the wintertime $300, $400 a month for electric and gas bills. Then bought food, kept my kids in clothes. How you supposed to save to get ahead with all that?

And the house, when we moved in the landlords said they'd do this and that, fix this and that. Said we would have an option to buy it. We said, "Okay, and we'll do these things." We had an agreement.

We never got that chance to buy, and they never fixed those things. But we kept paying that $950 a month. They had a barrel over us: we needed some place to go. And they made a small fortune those years. A month after we moved out we went by: all those things they wouldn't do were done.

Before that the guy decided to sell his house, just like that, and we had to move. It was December, wintertime. For a while we were staying with [Linda's] mother in a two-bedroom. Nine people. We had to be somewhere so we took that second place before we had even seen it.

Everybody has to have a place to live. And people will do what they have to do to survive. A lot of things that you see going on around here are for survival [he sweeps his hand, indicating the housing projects]. I'm not taking up for them, there's a lot of things happening here that I oppose. But where there's a will there's a way, you know.

Mexican Immigrants Face Poverty and Suffering

by Francisco Arguelles

Every year hundreds of thousands of Mexicans steal across the border into the United States. Most end up earning low wages harvesting crops in the Southwest. Some of these migrants choose to remain illegally in the United States because employment opportunities in Mexico are not as plentiful. Others work seasonally in America and then return to their families, who await the profits of their toil. In the following article, activist and educator Francisco Arguelles relates common experiences of Mexican migrants. He discusses the hardships that compel them to travel north across the border as well as the obstacles they face as they make the illegal crossing. Arguelles also describes the anguish of the family members left behind who must live in misery and poverty until their loved ones return.

Francisco Arguelles Paz y Puente was born in Mexico and began working with immigrants in Chiapas, Mexico, as an educator in 1983. He has since relocated to Houston, Texas, where he continues to fight for migrant rights. He is currently a board member of the National Network for Immigrant and Refugee Rights.

What the eyes see is a journey of dreams: Mountains and pine forests, small herds of goats and cows cared for by women and children, with big eyes and cheeks, red from the cold, the sun, and the dust. Farms that extend from one side to the other of the mountain range of the Nixcongo between the state of Mexico and the state of Morelos. The hidden houses between the cornfields and the foliage of the plum trees can be located by the smoke of the cooking ranges.

On a little hill apart from this shines the white chapel against the blue of the sky. That is where we got together with the women and children on Saturdays to study catechism, pray and try to understand life better.

What the eyes see when they look more closely is land eroded by excessive grazing and deforestation, rivers and wells dry or contaminated by excessive use of pesticides, plums and shawls that go to market without finding a fair price, young people who can't find work, old people who can't find medicine, children without school. What the eyes see is extreme poverty that is seen but not understood.

THE TALES OF HARDSHIP

In order to understand poverty, it is not enough to look. One must listen to those who survive it daily, and in order to listen, one must be quiet. This is what we did on one of our visits to the communities [when Arguelles was working with the Education for Peace project, a Catholic education service in Mexico]. What we listened to were sad stories that we were told, that Mario died, the youngest son of Antonio and Octavia, that he died from bronchitis, he died because the clinic was too far away. When they arrived at the clinic, the doctor wasn't there and they had to come back the next day. But during the night he got worse and they started out again, riding on the mule, but he died on the way, just like that, having lived fourteen months. He died of bronchitis and poverty.

Another story we listened to was that Maria couldn't come today to the meeting because her husband had been drunk for three days and yesterday he hit her, and if she goes out he will hit her again. Why is Juan drunk? Because next week he is going to the States to look for work because there is no work here and not enough money. The men always feel like drinking before they go, it gives them courage. But when they are drunk they often beat up their wives and children . . . then the women and children are shut up in their houses, too scared to leave or come to the meetings in the little church, because they don't want to leave the house or give fuel to gossip that their husbands might hear when they come back . . . if they come back.

We listened to the story of young men who risk their lives to help their families survive, men who conquer their fear of the unknown by trying to become hard.

THE CHALLENGES OF MIGRANT WORKERS AND THEIR FAMILIES

Eighty per cent of the young men go to the U.S. starting in January and don't come back until July or August, to harvest their cornfields.

While they are gone, the load of work multiplies for their wives and older children, who have to take care of the cornfields, fetch the water and the firewood, take care of the animals, take care of the sicknesses, and also live with the anguish of knowing that their husband or father or brother is far away and who knows how they might be doing.

These levels of anguish that challenge the migrants and their families are enormous and have negative effects on their physical and mental health. Many of the migrant workers that I have come to know in this region of Mexico have gastritis and insomnia and return to alcohol in order to get rid of the anxiety that the traumatic situations they go through during their journey and their time in the U.S. provokes in them.

The danger of crossing the border, like the gangs of assailants, the border patrol, the dangerous accidents that take place when they jump onto a moving train, the long walks in desert areas without food or water can turn into real traumas that severely affect the health, mental and physical, of those who suffer them. Also, it is not uncommon for them to develop grave difficulties in adjusting once more to their community, such as violent behavior with their family and neighbors. The humiliations, privations and aggressions suffered during the experience of migration can turn into aggression and violence when they return to their homes and don't have a chance to "integrate" everything they have experienced. Severe psychological problems, such as depression and postraumatic stress syndrome will never be recognized by name within a population that barely has access to basic health services and even less to psychiatric services or counseling.

The conflicts that become unleashed during the difficulties of readjustment after migration, the effects of violence on women and children, the men's bitterness because of the bad treatment they have received from their bosses, or because of being deported, the wounds from the work accidents, all of these "invisible" effects of migration last a long time in the communities, much longer than the money that the worker earns on the "other side.". . .

ENDURING STRIFE TO PROVIDE FOR THE FAMILY

If migration causes so much harm to the migrants, it is a valid question to ask, Why do they keep coming? Are they masochists maybe? Or is it simply because this is a valid way of survival in this complex world at the end of the [twentieth] century in which there are more and more poor people who have less and less?

I don't know. I do know that they don't come here because they like it. I do know that in their countries they don't have opportunities to progress, nor access to work or education, nor fair markets for their products, nor public services that would improve their quality of life. There are many things lacking.

But I also know that they have their faith, a profound faith that helps them carry all their problems and that could also be a great richness and seed of evangelization for the societies that have the good fortune to receive them—if they knew how to listen to them without remaining blind to the challenge and treasure that God has put into their hands. Some groups do it, they have done it for many years and can testify to what God has done in them by way of these, his favorite and smallest children.

This faith in a God of Love that helps the poor to survive, and those who receive them to be open, needs to be complemented by community action that allows the migrants and their families to integrate all the suffering and anguish that is a part of migration, and also to harvest the positive fruits of being far away from one's loved ones and encountering them again.

An Asian Immigrant Faces Harsh Working Conditions

by Lisa Liu, interviewed by David Bacon

Lisa Liu is a garment worker living in Oakland, California. Having come from China to America, she is a member of California's large Asian migrant-worker culture. Much of her time is spent working as a seamstress in a Chinatown factory. In the following interview with David Bacon, Liu describes the conditions within her factory. Her days are characterized by long, hard hours of piecework with almost no breaks, low pay, and little sympathy from supervisors. Liu and some of her fellow workers made the decision to organize to petition the factory bosses to improve such conditions.

While in China, Liu explains, she endured the trials of living under the strict rules of the government and longed for the freedoms embodied by the American way of life. Upon coming to the United States, however, her dreams soon evaporated as she became one of the faceless and voiceless individuals of the American working poor. Liu tells of the difficulties she faces in living without health insurance, overcoming the language barrier, and making ends meet on an income that at times is less than the governmentally mandated minimum wage. Liu fails to see much of a difference between her life under the rule of Chinese communism and her struggle for freedom in America.

David Bacon is a journalist and photographer who writes stories and does photo exhibits on labor and immigration topics. He has also been a labor organizer for two decades.

I'm a seamstress in a factory with twelve other people. We sew children's clothes—shirts and dresses. I've worked in the garment industry here for twelve years, and at the factory where I am now for over a year.

In our factory we have to work ten hours a day, six to seven days a week. The contractor doesn't pay us any benefits—no health

Lisa Liu, interviewed by David Bacon, "The Story of a Garment Worker," *Dollars & Sense*, September/October 2000, pp. 11–12. Copyright © 2000 by David Bacon. Reproduced by permission.

insurance or vacations. While we get a half-hour for lunch, there are no other paid breaks in our shift.

We get paid by the piece, and count up the pieces to see what we make. If we work faster we get paid more. But if the work is difficult and the manufacturer gives the contractor a low price, then what we get drops so low that maybe we'll get forty dollars a day. The government says the minimum wage is $5.75, but I don't think that by the piece we can reach $5.75 an hour a lot of the time.

When we hurt from the work we often just feel it's because of our age. People don't know that over the years their working posture can cause lots of pain. We just take it for granted, and in any case there's no insurance to pay for anything different. We just wait for the pain to go away.

BONDING TOGETHER

That's why we organize the women together and have them speak out their problems at each of the garment shops. If we stop being silent about these things, we can demand justice. We can get paid hourly and bring better working conditions to the workers.

Our idea is to tell them how to fight for their rights and explain what rights they have. Everyone should know more about the laws. We let them know about the minimum wage and that there should be breaks after four hours of work. We organize classes to teach women that we can be hurt from work. And we've opened up a worker's clinic to provide medical treatment and diagnosis. We do this work with the help of Asian Immigrant Women Advocates here in Chinatown.

We can't actually speak to the manufacturers whose clothes we're sewing because they don't come down to the shops to listen to the workers. So when we have a problem it's difficult to bring it to them. Still, we've had campaigns where we got the manufacturer to pay back-wages to the workers after the contractor closed without paying them. We got a hotline then, for workers to complain directly to the manufacturers. That solved some problems. The fire doors in those shops aren't blocked anymore, and the hygiene is better.

But it's not easy for women in our situation, and many are scared. Because they only work in the Chinese community, they're afraid their names will become known to the community and the bosses will not hire them. That's why we try to do things together. There's really no other place for us to go. Most of us don't have the training or the skills to work in other industries. We mostly speak just one language, usually Cantonese, and often just the dialect Toishanese.

REALIZING THE TRUTH ABOUT THE AMERICAN DREAM

When I first came to the United States I needed a lot of time to work to stabilize myself. So after seven years that's why I'm only now having my first baby. We don't have any health insurance and we have to pay the bill out of our own pockets. Health insurance is very expensive in the United States. We can't afford it. In the garment industry here they do not have health insurance for the workers.

Before I came here, my experience in China was that life was very strict. I heard that in America you have a lot of freedom, and I wanted to breathe the air of that freedom. But when I came here I realized the reality was very different from what I had been dreaming, because my idea of freedom was very abstract. I thought that freedom was being able to choose the place where you work. If you don't like one place, you can go work in another. In China you cannot do this. When you get assigned to a post, you have to work at that post.

Since I've come to the United States, I feel like I cannot get into the mainstream. There's a gap, like I don't know the background of American history and the laws. And I don't speak English. So I can only live within Chinatown and the Chinese community and feel scared. I cannot find a good job, so I have to work the low-income work. So I learned to compare life here and in China in a different way.

Many people say life here is very free. But for us, it's a lot of pressure. You have to pay rent, living costs so much money, you have all kinds of insurance—car insurance, health insurance, life insurance—that you can't afford. With all that kind of pressure, sometimes I feel I cannot breathe.

Everywhere you go you just find low pay. All the shops pay by the piece, and they have very strict rules. You cannot go to the bathroom unless it's lunch time. Some places they put up a sign that says, "Don't talk while you work." You're not allowed to listen to the radio.

Wherever you go, in all the garment factories, the conditions and the prices are almost the same. The boss says, "I cannot raise the price for you and if you complain any more, then just take a break tomorrow—don't come to work." So even though I can go from one job to another, where's the freedom?

74

Work Does Not Necessarily End Poverty

by Marion Graham

In the following narrative, Marion Graham, an ex-welfare mother and cofounder of Advocacy for Resources for Modern Survival (ARMS), a welfare advocacy group, gives an account of her experiences as a member of America's working poor. She raised five children while receiving state assistance, but eventually decided to return to work in order to provide a better quality of life for her kids. Graham claims to have misjudged the positive aspects of weaning her family off welfare because she soon realized that having a job does not necessarily mean an end to financial hardship. Although a job does provide her a steady source of income, a working life entails many expenses. For example, the costs of commuting to and from her job as an administrative assistant at the University of Massachusetts (Boston), employee health insurance, and retirement benefits all subtract from her gross income. Graham thus finds herself with more expenses than she had while on welfare yet not enough income to meet them. She defines such a circumstance as "invisible poverty," or the state of having an income yet still hovering around the poverty line.

I was born in Boston, the youngest of a four-girl family. When I was 13, my father's firm went bankrupt and he found himself out of a job. My family were so ashamed they wouldn't tell their friends that they had to move from the suburbs to a three-decker in Boston, even though they weren't really poor. Now I know a lot of people who would love to move out of the projects into a three-decker.

In 1960 I got married. I left my good job with the telephone company when I was pregnant with my first child, in 1961. I really looked forward to being home with my children. Nobody worked that I knew. During the '60s I was always pregnant when everybody was

Marion Graham, *For Crying Out Loud: Women's Poverty in the United States*, edited by Diane Dujon and Ann Withorn. Cambridge, MA: South End Press, 1996. Copyright © 1996 by Diane Dujon and Ann Withorn. Reproduced by permission.

out rebelling against everything. I was too pregnant to rebel, so I have to rebel now! I have five kids. They are now 35, 32, 31, 30, and 27.

When I saw how my marriage was disintegrating, I did work at home for marketing research companies, and I did typing for college students, just to try to make money. I had planned for two or three years to get a divorce before I did. But I never had the money to do it. I knew I had to have a job in order to save the money to go to a lawyer. I couldn't leave the kids; there was no daycare. Finally, I had to go on welfare because my husband did not pay enough support, and sometimes he did not pay at all.

When I started working full-time again, I thought it was going to be wonderful, that I wasn't going to be poor anymore. I was going to be away from the bureaucracy; they couldn't call me in anytime they wanted to. Even then, though, I still earned so little that I was eligible for a housing subsidy, Medicaid, and food stamps. I remember at the time being ashamed to let people where I worked know that I was poor enough for food stamps. And I hated that.

WORKING BUT STILL POOR

About three years ago they came out with some new "poverty line," that's what they called it, and they decided I earned too much for most of those other benefits. I only grossed something like $8,600 at the time, but it was still too much for them, so they cut me off. I still had the same needs I had before, but suddenly I was no longer poor. I guess I was supposed to be proud.

Since then I got a raise, so I thought things would be O.K., but then I lost my housing subsidy because I earned too much. I ended up having to take an apartment that cost exactly seven times what I had paid with a subsidy. My rent came to half of my net pay. Just the rent. After that sometimes I would get to work but not be able to pay for lunch. I had my subway tokens, but no money to eat. Every week they take something different out of my salary. Life insurance, disability insurance, union dues, retirement benefits are all good, but you don't get much to live on. Now, finally, I can buy *Woman's Day* and *Family Circle* magazines—that used to be my dream.

How you dress for work, the hours and flexibility, transportation, whether you can bring a lunch—all these nitty-gritty things make a big difference in how you can live on a low salary. You just cannot afford to take some jobs even if they sound interesting because you have to spend too much money on clothes or transportation. It's sad. I couldn't afford to work at a place where I had to dress up, for instance. You can't "dress for success" on a secretarial salary. It's an invisible poverty.

You think you're not poor because you are working, so you don't even ask for the information about benefits you need. And nobody tells you that you might be eligible, because they think you are working and all set. Also, it is even harder to ask for things from your family, because if you are working you should have the money. I feel bad, though, that I don't have more chance to help my family. I can't afford it, even though I'm working.

The average pay in my union of clerical and hospital workers is not much above poverty for a woman who is trying to raise a family. When people need childcare they have to pay for it, and they can't afford it. I don't need childcare, but the health insurance, which I had to wait two years for, costs a lot. And I couldn't get it for my son, who has suffered from juvenile diabetes since he was very young.

THE STIGMA OF WELFARE

Not having money affects everything about how you feel. I used to feel lousy about myself. I thought I was supposed to be set, to have a slice of the American pie. Now I was a big person and I worked and everything, and I was supposed to get there. But instead I found myself just with a job and no money. When I reached 40 I was so depressed.

Now I have learned that I am not alone, that it is not my fault. The average secretary around here is just over the line for many benefits, but we still have expenses we can't meet. That makes some women, who don't understand how it works, take it out on women on welfare. They blame them for getting something they can't have, instead of blaming the rules, which keep them from getting anything. Some secretaries may think, "I am better off than they are," instead of seeing how we have similar problems. But they are afraid of the label that would be put on them if they identified with welfare. I don't do that because I have been there and I know both, and I know that none of it is good. It's bad to be on welfare, and it is bad to be working and have no money.

As secretaries here we have worked hard to do things together so that we can know each other as people, because at work we are all separated in our individual little offices. We go on picnics together, or to dinner, just to get to know each other. Although they don't pay us much, they act like we can never be absent or the world will fall apart, so we have to cover for each other, and we can't do that if we don't know each other. I keep saying, "If we are so important, why don't they pay us more?" But they don't, so we have to help each other.

CHAPTER 4

Helping the Poor

A Nun Learns from the Third World Poor

by Ellen Rufft

Ellen Rufft is a Catholic nun and former director of the Pittsburgh Province of the Sisters of Divine Providence. She has written many articles for *America* magazine, a weekly Catholic periodical. In the following article, Rufft explains how she was initially wary of accepting an opportunity to visit the Caribbean island of Santo Domingo with convent missionaries. According to Rufft, she was afraid of how she might behave in a country whose people are so impoverished. After making the journey, however, her attitude changed. Although distraught at the islanders' living conditions, she was pleasantly surprised by their gracious support of the church and their personable human warmth. The experience led her to recognize an important life lesson: that those who have money are no different than those who do not, except that the well-off have more options than people in need.

I used to like the idea of placing all people into one of two groups: the brave or the fainthearted. I willingly put myself in the latter category and therefore felt justified in not doing many things that only "brave" people do: being a missionary, going to jail to protest some injustice, or even traveling to a third world country. When I was invited to visit our sisters who had begun a mission in Santo Domingo, I did not want to go. It wasn't that I did not want to see the work our community was doing there, but rather that I fit so well into category two! I was afraid I would get sick on the food, embarrass myself by my fear of rats, not know what to say to or how to help people in need. I was especially concerned about the images of poverty that I knew would remain with me after my visit.

Pictures of such scenes from movies, television, and magazines continually haunt me and leave me with feelings of impotence and a vague guilt. I was worried that, after seeing so much misery in person,

I would have an even heavier sense of helplessness and be plagued by greater guilt for not doing more to relieve the burdens of the people in the Dominican Republic and other third world countries.

UNPREPARED FOR THE PEOPLE

It was, in many ways, as I had feared. On the first day of my visit, the sisters took me down a long, steep dirt hill that wound in and out of dilapidated shacks and led to a school for little children that one of the sisters administers. It was impossible not to notice the river down there, polluted with garbage and raw sewage, the naked children with distended stomachs and orange hair from malnutrition, the rats. I could not escape the smells; it was difficult not to retch. In a way that mattered most, however, it was not at all as I had expected. I was unprepared for the people! I had steeled myself to witness heart-rending scenes of poverty, but I was not ready for the people!

We went to Mass the first evening I was in Santo Domingo, and they were there—in their church clothes, their one good dress or shirt, perhaps with a hole or two, but spotlessly clean. They were there rushing to welcome us, the strangers, with warm embraces as if they knew us. They were there praying and singing with the fervor of those who believe that God is truly listening. They were there with their children, smiling as the little ones roamed in and out of the makeshift benches, pausing often to climb onto the laps of those who welcomed them. They were there as we left the little church, thanking us for coming and begging us to return. And they are there still, unaware of how little I was prepared to meet them.

THEY ARE JUST LIKE US, AND NOT LIKE US

It was not until I was back home, still thinking about them, that I understood why they had caught me so off guard. It was the awareness that came to me almost as a shock when I saw them together in church: they are people just like us. Of course I have always known intellectually that people are basically the same everywhere, but I had never experienced it in such a dramatic way. It was clear to me in that little church building that these people think, feel and believe in much the same way we do, in their affection for one another, in their hospitality to strangers, in their love of children, in the value they place on cleanliness, in their desire to worship together.

What makes them different from us is none of those basic human characteristics; it is rather that we have many options in our lives, and they have very few. They cannot decide, as I could, if they are "brave" enough to visit a third world country; they live in one. They cannot choose which type of washing machine to buy; they have only plastic buckets with cold water from rusty pipes sticking out of the ground. For them, there is no decision about whether or not to go to Weight Watchers to take off a few pounds, they spend much of their time trying to find enough food to keep themselves and their children alive. They have few options about where they live, what they wear, how much they eat or what their future will be.

My heightened awareness of the choices I have in my life, choices denied to many people in the world, ought to have increased my feelings of helplessness and guilt. It has, instead, become a potent reminder that what is mine is not so by right. It has motivated me to use the many options I am given with a greater awareness of those who have fewer. Because that consciousness tends to wane with time, I have an opportunity to remember those who have no choice about which flavor of ice cream to eat, for example, by having none myself.

I WANT TO REMEMBER

My memory of those families who live in one small sweltering room stays more alive when I occasionally choose not to put on the air conditioning in the car on a hot day. I do not think such choices make the lives of those with limited options any better; I do them for me, so that I won't forget. I want to remember.

I want to remember so that from now on I make wiser, more compassionate choices in my life. When I returned from Santo Domingo, a friend said she was concerned that I would never be the same. I told her that my fear was that I would be. I pray daily that I am not.

A Psychiatrist Learns How to Help the Homeless

by Sara Forman

> In the following narrative, Sara Forman, a psychiatric trainee, writes of her experiences treating homeless patients in an urban center in England. Forman admits that a shabby work environment coupled with the unusual and even confusing needs of the poor made her initially uncomfortable with her training assignment. As Forman relates, however, dealing with the special needs of the homeless taught her many valuable lessons. She learned how to spot deceptive patients, how to treat more than just the mental health of her charges, and how to approach her patients with humility and respect. Above all, though, Forman recognized that her services—along with the services of other voluntary relief organizations—were helping to ease some of the burden of the homeless.

It came as no surprise to be told that my next placement as a psychiatric trainee would mean spending one session a week providing a consultation and liaison service to a general practice. I was a little surprised, however, to discover how few of my friends and colleagues knew the exact location of the surgery [doctor's office] to which I was assigned, though it was reputed to be only a stone's throw from the city centre.

On the appointed morning I followed the directions precisely, but on arrival I wondered whether I had been the victim of a complicated joke. Could this shabby portakabin [trailer] with its wire protected windows and graffiti splattered walls be the surgery? I parked gingerly, trying to avoid slashing my tyres on the debris of broken bottles. My attempt to manoeuvre my car into the tiny space provided was carried out under the good humoured but slightly mocking scrutiny of a group of men huddled together, sharing roll up cigarettes. One of the group stepped forward and introduced himself as the receptionist.

Sara Forman, "No Fixed Abode," *British Medical Journal*, vol. 304, May 2, 1992, p. 1,185. Copyright © 1992 by the British Medical Association. Reproduced by permission.

I was shown my consulting room, which doubled both as a storage area and as a treatment room. A couch, a chair, and numerous boxes took up most of the available floor space. There was a wash basin, but on that frozen February morning there was no running water and precious little heat. Water was brought from the next door building by eager volunteers.

Before long it became clear that not all the patients were waiting to be seen by a doctor or nurse. Some had come merely for the coffee, the company, or the warmth. For this was no ordinary surgery. Its clientele was, and is, composed entirely of the homeless. Here I would learn, over the next six months, to practise ordinary psychiatry in an extraordinary setting.

SHEDDING PRECONCEPTIONS ABOUT THE HOMELESS

Here too I learnt to discard my preconceived ideas about the needs and problems of the homeless. My new patients were not all schizophrenic or alcoholic, but presented a range of problems almost as diverse as that found in most general psychiatric outpatient clinics. Neat neuroses, however, were in the minority—people with phobias and the chronically anxious would not survive long on the streets, though some gravitated to the hostels for the homeless also served by the practice.

Reaching a diagnosis was often secondary to the mammoth task of unravelling the complex personal and social circumstances enmeshing and sometimes obscuring symptoms. Diagnostic manuals often seemed remote and rather unhelpful when faced with a paranoid patient, crawling with body lice, who had failed to persuade the Department of Social Security to replace his infested clothes, or a depressed man who had progressively lost his job, home, family, and self respect and had little prospect of regaining any of them. Terms such as "self neglect" and "low self esteem" took on additional layers of meaning in such circumstances.

Other cherished fragments of psychiatric terminology came in for reappraisal outside the cloister of the hospital. Multidisciplinary work became a livelier and less theoretical concept as I discovered that no depot injection [i.e., injections of antipsychotic drugs used to treat mental illness] can be given to a homeless person without the special skills required to find the recipient and persuade him to stay in one place long enough for needle and patient to make contact. Such skills do not belong exclusively to professionally trained staff: often it would be a receptionist who would access the network and provide the vital clues and contacts.

FLEXIBLE TREATMENT METHODS

The good natured banter over mugs of tea in the waiting area sometimes bore an uncanny resemblance to the informal supportive group therapy I had encountered only in wards and day hospitals.

Treatment methods often had to be adapted drastically in my new working environment, and I learnt some valuable lessons. If anyone had told me before my placement that it was possible to practise psychotherapy in a far from soundproof room with fights between drunken adversaries taking place only yards away I would have been incredulous. Now I know better. Similarly, I would have thought it impossible to adapt the diary keeping methods so beloved of cognitive behavioural therapists to the needs of a semiliterate patient whose written offerings were barely legible. I now know that motivation and a sense of humour, shared by patient and therapist, can move mountains of purist theory and achieve results.

Other lessons were less pleasant. I soon realised that medication was not necessarily swallowed by the recipient I had in mind. Money being in short supply, medication takes its place alongside alcohol and stolen goods in the alternative economy of the disadvantaged. This can lead to interesting diagnostic puzzles—continuing symptoms may be due to selling rather than swallowing tablets, and new symptoms may be the result of sampling a handful of mixed pills intended for quite different people and problems. Prescriptions got lost or stolen, and I learnt that cynicism and close communication with pharmacies were more appropriate responses than automatic sympathy when faced with requests for replacement prescriptions.

In time I also realised that I was sharpening my skill at differentiating between genuine psychiatric distress and extremely good acting by people whose only experience of warmth and comfort in recent years had been obtained in mental hospitals around the country.

LEARNING FROM MISTAKES

Although community based detoxification from alcohol was well developed and widely used, hospital treatment was occasionally required for acute withdrawal symptoms. On one such occasion I triumphantly secured a bed after prolonged telephone negotiation with a hard pressed hospital colleague, only to discover later that the patient had stopped en route to hospital for one last drink, or two or three. My failure to organise transport and escort had turned my short lived triumph into a farce. We learn by our mistakes.

Another memorable early mistake was to ask a new homeless patient for his address. Quick as a flash, he replied "Cloud cuckoo land," and showed his exasperation at being asked such an inadvertently tactless question by whipping a razor blade from his pocket and slashing his wrists in front of me.

These, and many other memorable experiences, taught me to begin to adapt my skills to the needs of patients whose histories often seemed to be chronic catalogues of adverse life events. Treatments could often be effective in the short term; longer term follow up was often difficult and unrewarding in a population whose whereabouts for the next week was not always predictable, let alone the next month. Prevention seemed like an unattainable luxury item on an otherwise basic menu of possible interventions, though occasionally my medical support of a housing application or of an application for a place on a rehabilitative work programme brought satisfactory rewards.

Before my attachment I was already intellectually convinced of the aetiological [causal] dangers of homelessness—homeless people are more vulnerable than the housed to the risk factors of unemployment, poverty, and lack of close, enduring relationships. I heard many detailed accounts of the interaction between homelessness and mental illness, and my previous intellectual conviction took on a new and personal dimension.

While homelessness is clearly bad for you, the experience of working with the homeless is good for you if you are a psychiatric trainee. It teaches you adaptability, humility, and immense respect for the voluntary organisations without whose efforts the plight of the homeless would be even worse than it already is, and even the most appalling on call doctor's accommodation seems tolerable after six month's exposure to the living conditions of those who have no fixed abode.

Helping the Homeless Help Themselves

by Doug Castle

SHARE (Seattle Housing And Resource Effort) is an advocacy organization run by homeless people in Seattle, Washington. In the early 1990s SHARE received permission from the local community to erect a temporary tent city to house impoverished individuals who were living on the streets. Doug Castle was sleeping under a bridge in Seattle when he heard of the tent city. Deciding to check it out, Castle became enamored with the do-it-yourself ethics of SHARE and quickly found a paid position in the organization.

In the following article from Steven VanderStaay's book *Street Lives*, Castle explains how SHARE offers homeless people both a place to stay and a means to restructure their lives. The program has stringent rules and restrictions, Castle notes, and the people who seek shelter in SHARE have to be committed to changing their lives by contributing to the community, finding employment, and saving money. The goal is for the homeless to temporarily avail themselves of SHARE's services and then transition into more permanent housing and a less rootless lifestyle. Castle believes that the SHARE program is effective in giving people a chance to get off the streets, and he is proud of the fact that the organization has showed the community that the homeless are willing to lift themselves out of their dire circumstances if given the chance.

SHARE means Seattle Housing And Resource Effort. There is no agency that is SHARE. Any person who believes that there is a homeless crisis, and that the solution must come from the efforts of homeless people rather than the government, can be a member of SHARE. There is no president, no dues, no board of directors.

I wasn't involved until tent city. This was late November [1990], right after Thanksgiving. All the shelters were full and it got around

Steven VanderStaay, *Street Lives: An Oral History of Homeless Americans*. Philadelphia, PA: New Society, 1992. Copyright © 1992 by Steven VanderStaay. Reproduced by permission of the author.

on the streets that that's where everybody was going, so I walked on down. There were 39 people living in 5 tents. I'm a big camping enthusiast and know a lot about tents, so I started helping out. And, you know, it was either that or go back under the I-90 bridge. So I stayed.

Less than three weeks later we had 45 tents, 148 people—we were the third largest shelter in the state of Washington, and we were doing it in a mud field with tents.

COMMUNITY SUPPORT

I expected the community to be up in arms about it. But where I was just shocked is that we had all this community support. The community was feeding us, bringing us blankets, bringing us clothes. . . . We passed out five thousand sleeping bags and seven thousand coats, to homeless and low-income people down there. I mean people brought donations down by the truck load.

See people liked the idea that homeless people were looking for a helping hand, not a handout. I mean we were willing to get up and do something about our own future and were not going to be dependent upon social agencies to decide that future. That was the start, the key. Everything else just followed from that.

Because of our community support the city became forced to find an equitable solution and . . . well, the Metro bus barn was sitting vacant, so we got that as a transitional building. The deal was, if we could run things for ourselves, the city would find us a permanent location.

Realistically, I don't believe the city expected us to succeed. That way once we'd failed they could come in, say "Oh this place is too whatever." You know, too many fights, too many drunks, too much neighborhood impact. Then they'd say, "Hey we tried, but the homeless people can't do it."

We surprised everybody. We got the panhandlers to go somewhere else. Every other Saturday we'd average fifty big black trash bags full of trash, cleaning up the area. It wasn't even our trash, but it proved a point: we were saying, "We're solving our own problem. Now unless you can come up with a better solution, just let us do our thing."

Not that there wasn't problems. The third day we were in the bus barn we had a fight between six people, four of them men, two of them women. In the process of getting this fight broke up, I got my nose broken, I got five stitches in my eyes, a detached retina, and a concussion. Spent the night in the hospital. And like I said this was the third night the bus barn was open.

WE DO IT ALL

It was chaos, and everybody in the place knew it. Everybody knew we weren't going to make the month of December if we didn't do something. But that's what I think is so remarkable, what we did: we voted ourselves the toughest set of rules of any shelter anywhere. And we chose it for ourselves. No sociologist making sixty-thousand a year crammed it down our throats. And that's why it worked. And because it worked the city was forced to come through on their word. That's how we got this place, the Aloha Hotel.

Back in tent city, the bus barn, even here today, we have had 24-hour security—all done internally, by homeless people. Everyone works: we man our own telephones, we prepare our own meals, wash our own clothes. Only three of us are paid. Myself, I make $150 a week for the 96 hours I spend on the job, but it's worth it for me because we put people into jobs and homes. I know how important that is because I know what it means to be homeless.

Our target population are single men, 25 to 40 years old. We're not exclusionary, but that's our target population, the group that has no other place to turn. And if you divide the homeless into the 30 percent drug or alcohol addicted, 30 percent mentally ill, and 30 percent down and out for situational reasons, the last 30 percent is the one we're after: people we believe can function in society if they're given some transitional help in getting reestablished.

But if someone's action plan includes drug or alcohol rehabilitation we'll accept that. As long as it's part of their success plan we're more than cooperative. See we give you 90 days. If we give you those 90 days we want to know what you can do with it. What will be your action steps financially, employmentwise, housingwise, and your other personal goals?

You have to line out a personal success plan and you're required to show that you're working on it. You're required to save $75 a week, you're required to put in 15 hours a week of work around here, and you're required to pay $5 a week for room and board. If you can't find the work yourself, we'll find it for you. Lots of our residents find each other jobs. They find a job, come back the next day and say, "Hey, they need two more people!" But you have to save that money, and you have to follow the rules.

POVERTY

It takes dedication to make this work. But it works. Already we're running a 50 percent success rate. Our first 90 days isn't even up—it won't be up until this weekend. But of the original 30 we moved in with, 15 have already moved on to some form of permanent housing. Another 6 or 7 have been thrown out for rules infractions. The idea there is not to waste time on people we can't help—or who won't help themselves. 'Cause this is not a flophouse. We need flophouses, I mean people deserve a bed, but there are other places for that. But if someone's willing to work to help himself, he deserves more. That's what we're here for.

This way we can free up bed spaces in shelters and help that 30 percent we're shooting at. And this kind of concept can work anywhere in America because there are homeless people who want out everywhere. We've even had Canadians come down and do interviews here; they're interested in starting this kind of program there.

TURNING LIVES AROUND

Our success goes back to our stringent rules, the 90 days we offer, and the people we work with. By and large, these people just want a chance, and they're willing to scratch and claw every inch. They make that inch and they go for another. You give 'em that break and they'll work for it.

It's a way of getting back in control of your life. Little things, like running our desk or being security around here, it gives you a sense that you're doing a job well done. That helps your self-worth. A lot of these people come in with a poor outlook on things and it just turns them around.

We had this woman, Crissy, who came to us pregnant. Shy, quiet, and timid. I mean all she had was a garbage bag with some clothes in it and the baby she was carrying. She had been a dispatcher for one of the cab companies. Then her husband skipped town, and that cost her where she was living. Eventually she lost everything: house, family, job, then her kids were taken away from her because she was homeless.

At the bus barn she helped run our desk. Then when we moved over here, she was on the executive committee, the screening committee, head of the desk, and probably the only person that got less sleep than me. She was here two months and when she left she was a fireball. Nothing was going to stop her. At that point she had a car, two vanloads of stuff, $700 in the bank, and an apartment.

90

Then this couple we had, they just moved out. He's disabled, and they had been living on the street for I don't know how long. But we helped him receive Social Security, she got a job, and they saved up the money until they could get an apartment over in Freemont. It's not public housing or anything. And she was able to get a son back that she had lost. Just one big happy family.

THE HOMELESS ARE PEOPLE WHO NEED HELP

See, it doesn't take paying somebody $60,000 a year to run a transitional house like this. A man making $60,000 a year, that has never been homeless, what does he know? There are people among the homeless who can do it. And it's more cost-effective if they do.

Most homeless people are intelligent. Many have some college education. I have two years of training in audio-engineering; I used to be the sound man and assistant manager for one of the largest nightclubs in NYC. But when people saw me living under a bridge, they just assumed that I'd always been living under that bridge.

Once you get that far down, where you're worrying about your absolute day-to-day survival . . . believe me I could take you around and let you stand in some of the food lines, let you stand in some of the clothing lines, and you will see that it will take up all of your day. You don't have time to go job hunting, you don't have time to worry about staying clean. You're worrying about putting a roof over your head that night and putting a meal in your belly. And due to the bureaucracy and red tape it takes to get those things, that's all you have time for.

See, to be an ally to a homeless person is very simple: approach him with an open mind and listen to his story. Don't listen with the idea that he's a typical Terry the Tramp—listen to him as a person.

And don't go to a bureaucrat for answers; ask a homeless person what he needs, and what he can do with your help. And let us in your neighborhoods. You know, if we can put a good program together, accept us in your neighborhood.

I mean, to start, people are gonna need clean clothes, a hot shower, and a place to sleep. Now some people who are homeless— lots of society—if you covered those needs that's all they want. But others, all that's going to do is jump start 'em enough to want more. And that's where we come in.

The Moral Dilemma of Giving Alms

by Daniel T. Wackerman

In the following narrative, Daniel T. Wackerman argues that almsgiving to panhandlers is not a guilt-free decision for most people, including himself. Wackerman states that he does what he can to be charitable to street beggars, but he is aware that his own contributions are limited by his finances. He also recognizes that his donations are not always the result of charity. He maintains that fear of being hassled as well as the desire to atone for personal failings at work or at home often motivate his giving. Though he is determined to remain charitable to the less fortunate, all of these factors have made Wackerman selective in choosing those street people to whom he will regularly donate his spare change. Daniel T. Wackerman wrote of his experiences in *America*, a national Catholic weekly magazine.

Somewhere between two Pennsylvania mountains, during a solitary drive home, I lost all radio reception. So, left with just myself, the road and the first snow of the season—a dreaded fate, no doubt, for a citizen of that generation with enmity for interiority—I tried to provide myself with a little music from memory.

My borrowed jalopy had a certain beat of its own—a distinct cycle of pings and squeaks whose rhythm, I soon discovered, could be regulated by my foot on the accelerator. But this rhythm was not conducive to my preferred, up-tempo fare—Elvis Costello, Pearl Jam or R.E.M.—and I was in no mood to serenade myself with oldies. I opted, then, for a music that could be humorous, poignant, nostalgic and suited to my Manhattan destination—old show tunes, of course.

About a third of the way through my admittedly limited repertoire, I found myself humming the final number from the Broadway musical "West Side Story," and I suddenly remembered—the way one remembers a previous night's disturbing dream—the last time I heard that song.

Daniel T. Wackerman, "Mind's Eye: The Only Thing I Could Do Was to Keep Singing My Song and Hope I Make the Right Decision," *America*, vol. 173, December 2, 1995, p. 6. Copyright © 1995 by America Press, www.americamagazine .org. All rights reserved. Reproduced by permission.

There is an old woman whose path I cross on certain days, when, to avoid the cold and rain, I choose the underground route to work from my subway stop. She stands at the 57th Street Metro exit and holds a cup out for spare change; but instead of begging, she sings old show tunes in a strong New Yorkese that suggests she must once have had a lovely singing voice. She is almost blind. I don't think she's homeless, though—probably an inhabitant of government-run housing. Sane and sober, she does not seem unhappy, just a little tired and hungry and cold.

She always stops singing to thank me after I make a small donation. Occasionally she asks for my name; on one occasion she wanted to know if I was Jewish. Then I continue on my way to work as she starts another tune that quickly fades amid the sounds of shoes on pavement, taxis and buses, men selling fruit.

THE PROBLEMS OF GIVING MONEY ON THE STREETS

I do not hold out my almsgiving for praise, but rather for scrutiny. As any urbanite knows, giving money on the street poses a few problems, the first of which is lack of funding. When I initially came to New York, I made an early effort to give money or food to any passer-by who made the request. But I soon had to give this up as impractical, as I realized that the number of requests far outweighed my financial capacity to assist. Then began that tricky calculation of when and when not to apply Christian charity.

If truth be told, the old practice of emptying my pockets of change and the occasional single bill was not always inspired by love for my fellow man. In certain neighborhoods I used to pass through, it was fear that had me scrounging for quarters—sometimes even before I encountered a request. And then there are those relentless beggars for whom a small bribe seems the perfect remedy. This too is a form of fear, I suppose—the fear of having one's peace interrupted.

GIVING OUT OF GUILT

A healthy sense of guilt can also be a kind of inspiration. Giving out of guilt is very much like giving out of fear. It is a kind of bribe to one's self that can temporarily massage that nagging ache of recent transgression. I am amazed at the beauty one can see upon the face of an anonymous street-dweller moments after fighting with a loved one or close friend. The problem here, of course, is that one's charity is based on that fickle personal barometer we call mood. We can make amends to our friend or loved one and, having gained the requisite forgiveness, pass nonchalantly by that not-so-beautiful-anymore beggar's face without pity's slightest pang.

Guilt is also assuaged by a little urban experience. Once, two blocks from my apartment door, I witnessed two youngish panhandlers in a heated argument over the lucrative turf outside a coffee shop. Moments later, the victor in this pathetic squabble—who so ably defended his territory—knelt in supplication with a shaking hand outstretched to elderly restaurant patrons, many of whom undoubtedly live on fixed incomes and social security. And there are always those who are begging just to support an addiction to alcohol or other drugs.

So, like most of my fellow city-dwellers, I pick and choose who will receive my street alms. I have a few regulars, like my forgotten Broadway singer, who I trust won't run into the nearest liquor store for a pint. For others who meet my rather inexact standards, I'll occasionally buy a bit of food or some hot coffee—but no more money.

Thus I thought and hummed my way the length of Interstate 80 without the assistance of a radio. I knew that after I crossed the bridge and started toward my New York neighborhood I'd be faced with desperate men rushing out at red lights to wash my dirty windshield, who'd berate me if I did not open my window and give something. Perhaps when I finally found a parking spot on the street a woman would rush up as I locked my door and ask for money for diapers or formula. What would I do?

The only reasonable thing I could do without being smug and uncharitable, I thought, is to keep singing my song and hope I make the right decision. "There's a place for us. Somewhere, there's a place for us. . . ."

The editors have compiled the following list of organizations concerned with the issues debated in this book. The descriptions are derived from materials provided by the organizations. All have publications or information available for interested readers. The list was compiled on the date of publication of the present volume; the information provided here may change. Be aware that many organizations take several weeks or longer to respond to inquiries, so allow as much time as possible.

AMERICAN ENTERPRISE INSTITUTE FOR PUBLIC POLICY RESEARCH (AEI)

1150 Seventeenth St. NW, Washington, DC 20036
(202) 862-5800 • fax: (202) 862-7178
e-mail: info@aei.org • Web site: www.aei.org

The institution is dedicated to preserving and strengthening what it views as the foundations of freedom—limited government, private enterprise, vital cultural and political institutions, and a strong foreign policy and national defense—through scholarly research, open debate, and publications. AEI research covers economics and trade; social welfare; government tax, spending, regulatory, and legal policies; domestic policies; international affairs; defense; and foreign policies. The institute publishes dozens of books and hundreds of articles and reports each year as well as a policy magazine, the *American Enterprise.*

BOX PROJECT

100 Business Center Dr., Suite 26, Ormond Beach, FL 32174
(800) 268-9928 • fax: (386) 677-8617
e-mail: info@boxproject.org • Web site: www.boxproject.org

The Box Project is a national nonprofit organization founded in 1962. It seeks to help people in America's blighted rural areas by easing the effects of poverty and increasing the awareness of poverty. Programs such as Family Match assign volunteer sponsors to individuals and families living in poverty in rural America. The sponsors develop long-term friendships, provide encouragement, give advice, and donate boxes of needed supplies about once a month.

BROOKINGS INSTITUTION

1775 Massachusetts Ave. NW, Washington, DC 20036-2188
(202) 797-6000 • fax: (202) 797-6004
e-mail: brookinfo@brook.edu • Web site: www.brookings.edu

The Brookings Institution is devoted to nonpartisan research, education, and publication in economics, government, foreign policy, and the social sciences. Its principal purposes are to aid in the development of sound public policies and to promote public understanding of issues of national importance. It publishes the quarterly journal *Brookings Review,* which periodically includes articles on poverty, and numerous books, including *The Urban Underclass.*

CATO INSTITUTE

1000 Massachusetts Ave. NW, Washington, DC 20001-5403
(202) 842-0200 • fax: (202) 842-3490
e-mail: cato@cato.org • Web site: www.cato.org

The Cato Institute is a libertarian public policy research organization that advocates limited government. It has published articles on poverty in its quarterly *Cato Journal* and in its Policy Analysis series of papers.

CENTER FOR COMMUNITY CHANGE

1000 Wisconsin Ave. NW, Washington, DC 20007
(202) 342-0519
e-mail: info@communitychange.org • Web site: www.communitychange.org

The Center for Community Change helps low-income families build grassroots organizations to improve their communities and change public policy. The center provides support and resources to interested organizations committed to social change. It publishes a newsletter and various informational pamphlets on improving economic development, health care, and other issues concerning the poor.

CENTER FOR LAW AND SOCIAL POLICY (CLASP)

1015 Fifteenth St. NW, Suite 400, Washington, DC 20005
(202) 906-8000 • fax: (202) 842-2885
Web site: www.clasp.org

CLASP is a national nonprofit organization that seeks to improve the economic conditions of low-income families with children. The center analyzes federal and state policies and practices in the areas of welfare reform and workforce development. It produces materials designed to explain the meaning and implications of these policies and practices for federal, state, and local officials; community organizations; and service providers. CLASP produces numerous publications on issues related to family economic security and civil legal assistance that can be found on its Web site.

CENTER OF CONCERN

1225 Otis St. NE, Washington, DC 20017
(202) 635-2757 • fax: (202) 832-9494
e-mail: coc@coc.org • Web site: www.coc.org

The Center of Concern engages in social analysis, theological reflection, policy advocacy, and public education on issues of justice and peace. Its programs and writings include subjects such as international development, women's roles, economic alternatives, and a theology based on justice for all peoples. It publishes the bimonthly newsletter *Center Focus* as well as numerous papers and books, including *Opting for the Poor: A Challenge for North Americans.*

CENTER ON BUDGET AND POLICY PRIORITIES

820 First St. NE, Suite 510, Washington, DC 20002
(202) 408-1080 • fax: (202) 408-1056
e-mail: center@cbpp.org • Web site: www.cbpp.org

The center promotes better public understanding of the impact of federal and state governmental spending policies and programs primarily affecting low- and moderate-income Americans. It acts as a research center and information clearinghouse for the media, national and local organizations, and individuals. The center publishes numerous fact sheets, articles, and reports, including "The Safety Net Delivers: The Effects of Government Benefit Programs in Reducing Poverty."

CHILDREN'S DEFENSE FUND (CDF)

25 E St. NW, Washington, DC 20001
(202) 628-8787
e-mail: cdfinfo@childrensdefense.org • Web site: www.childrensdefense.org

CDF works to promote the interests of children in America. It pays particular attention to the needs of poor, minority, and disabled children. Its publications include *The State of America's Children 1998* and *Wasting America's Future: The Children's Defense Fund's Report on the Costs of Child Poverty.*

COALITION ON HUMAN NEEDS

1120 Connecticut Ave. NW, Suite 910, Washington, DC 20036
(202) 223-2532 • fax: (202) 223-2538
e-mail: chn@chn.org • Web site: www.chn.org

The coalition is a federal advocacy organization that works in such areas as federal budget and tax policy, housing, education, health care, and public assistance. It lobbies for adequate federal funding for welfare, Medicaid, and other social services. Its publications include *How the Poor Would Remedy Poverty*, the *Directory of National Human Needs Organizations*, and the biweekly legislative newsletter *Human Needs Report.*

CONGRESSIONAL HUNGER CENTER

229 Pennsylvania Ave. SE, Washington, DC 20003
(202) 547-7022 • fax: (202) 547-7575
Web site: www.hungercenter.org

The Congressional Hunger Center offers statistics on hunger and poverty, information about organizations dealing with international relief and development, contact information for charities, and service and volunteer opportunities.

ECONOMIC POLICY INSTITUTE (EPI)

1660 L St. NW, Suite 1200, Washington, DC 20036
(202) 775-8810 • (800) 374-4844 (publications)
(202) 331-5510 (Washington, DC) • fax: (202) 775-0819
e-mail: epi@epinet.org • Web site: www.epinet.org

EPI was established in 1986 to pursue research and public education to help define a new economic strategy for the United States. Its goal is to identify policies that can provide prosperous, fair, and balanced economic growth. It publishes numerous policy studies, briefing papers, and books, including *State of Working America* and *Declining American Incomes and Living Standards*.

HERITAGE FOUNDATION

214 Massachusetts Ave. NE, Washington, DC 20002-4999
(202) 546-4400 • fax: (202) 546-8328
e-mail: info@heritage.org • Web site: www.heritage.org

The Heritage Foundation is a public policy research institute dedicated to the principles of free competitive enterprise, limited government, individual liberty, and a strong national defense. The foundation publishes *Insider*, a monthly newsletter; *Heritage Today*, a newsletter published six times per year; and various reports and journals.

INSTITUTE FOR FOOD AND DEVELOPMENT POLICY

398 Sixtieth St., Oakland, CA 94618
(510) 654-4400 • fax: (510) 654-4551
e-mail: foodfirst@foodfirst.org • Web site: www.foodfirst.org

The institute is a research, documentation, and public education center focusing on the social and economic causes of world hunger. It believes that there is enough food in the world to adequately feed everyone, but hunger results "when people lack control over the resources they need to produce food." It publishes the quarterly *Food First Backgrounders* as well as numerous articles, pamphlets, and books, including *An Update of World Hunger: Twelve Myths*.

INSTITUTE FOR RESEARCH ON POVERTY (IRP)

University of Wisconsin-Madison
1180 Observatory Dr., 3412 Social Science Building, Madison, WI 53706-1393
(608) 262-6358 • fax: (608) 265-3119
e-mail: evanson@ssc.wisc.edu • Web site: www.ssc.wisc.edu/irp

The IRP is a national, university-based center for research into the causes and consequences of poverty and social inequality in the United States. It sponsors research and disseminates information by means of seminars, workshops, conferences, and a publications program that includes print and electronic products. The institute newsletter, *Focus*, discussion papers, and special reports are available online.

NATIONAL ALLIANCE TO END HOMELESSNESS

1518 K St. NW, Suite 410, Washington, DC 20005
(202) 638-1526 • fax: (202) 638-4664
e-mail: naeh@naeh.org • Web site: www.naeh.org

The alliance is a national organization committed to the ideal that no American should have to be homeless. It works to secure more effective national and local policies to aid the homeless. Its publications include *What You Can Do to Help the Homeless* and the monthly newsletter *Alliance*.

NATIONAL CENTER FOR CHILDREN IN POVERTY (NCCP)

215 W. 125th St., 3rd Fl., New York, NY 10027
(646) 284-9600 • fax: (646) 284-9623
e-mail: info@nccp.org • Web site: www.nccp.org

The center identifies and promotes strategies that prevent child poverty in the United States and that improve the lives of low-income children and their families. NCCP's social science research unit conducts original research and publishes reports that alert the nation to the threat posed by child poverty. In addition, the center publishes numerous reports, fact sheets, and opinion pieces and uses online communications and library-based resources to disseminate a broad array of research-based information that is relevant to improving children's lives. The center also commissions public opinion research to gain a deeper understanding of attitudes about child poverty and to gain insights into the attitudinal barriers that have prevented action to reduce child poverty.

NATIONAL COALITION FOR THE HOMELESS

2201 P St. NW, Washington, DC 20037
(202) 737-6444 • fax: (202) 737-6445
e-mail: info@nationalhomeless.org • Web site: www.nationalhomeless.org

The primary aim of the National Coalition for the Homeless is to end homelessness. Through grassroots organizations and education, the coalition influences governmental policy in four areas: housing justice, economic justice, health care justice, and civil rights. The organization also publishes a newsletter and maintains a current database for research into homelessness.

NATIONAL STUDENT CAMPAIGN AGAINST HUNGER AND HOMELESSNESS (NSCAHH)

233 N. Pleasant Ave., Amherst, MA 01002
(413) 253-6417 • fax: (413) 256-6435
e-mail: info@studentsagainsthunger.org • Web site: www.nscahh.org

NSCAHH is a network of college and high school students, educators, and community leaders who work to fight hunger and homelessness in the United States and around the world. Its mission is to create a generation of student/community activists who will explore and understand the root causes of poverty and who will initiate positive change through service and action. It publishes the quarterly newsletter *Students Making a Difference* as well as numerous manuals, fact sheets, and handbooks.

POVERTY AND RACE RESEARCH ACTION COUNCIL (PRRAC)

3000 Connecticut Ave. NW, Suite 200, Washington, DC 20008
(202) 387-9887 • fax: (202) 387-0764
e-mail: info@prrac.org • Web site: www.prrac.org

PRRAC was established by civil rights, antipoverty, and legal services groups. It works to develop antiracism and antipoverty strategies and provides funding for research projects that support advocacy work. It publishes the bimonthly newsletter *Poverty & Race.*

PROGRESSIVE POLICY INSTITUTE (PPI)

600 Pennsylvania Ave. SE, Suite 400, Washington, DC 20003
(202) 547-0001 • fax: (202) 544-5014
e-mail: webmaster@dlcppi.org • Web site: www.ppionline.org

PPI develops policy alternatives to the conventional liberal-conservative political debate. It advocates social policies that move beyond merely maintaining the poor to liberating them from poverty and dependency. Its publications include *Microenterprise: Human Reconstruction in America's Inner Cities* and *Social Service Vouchers: Bringing Choice and Competition to Social Services.*

SALVATION ARMY

615 Slaters Ln., PO Box 269, Alexandria, VA 22313
(703) 684-5500 • fax: (703) 684-3478
e-mail: SA_information@USN.salvationarmy.org
Web site: www.salvationarmyusa.org

The Salvation Army offers a wide variety of assistance to the less fortunate of the world. From drug rehabilitation to community development, the Christian organization strives to give a better way of life to the poor.

URBAN INSTITUTE

2100 M St. NW, Washington, DC 20037
(202) 833-7200
e-mail: paffairs@ui.urban.org • Web site: www.urban.org

The Urban Institute investigates social and economic problems confronting the nation and analyzes efforts to solve these problems. In addition, it works to improve government decisions and their implementations and to increase citizen awareness about important public choices. It offers a wide variety of resources, including books such as *Restructuring Medicare: Impacts on Beneficiaries.*

WELFARE INFORMATION NETWORK (WIN)

1401 New York Ave. NW, Suite 800, Washington, DC 20005
(202) 587-1000 • fax: (202) 628-4205
e-mail: bvlare@financeprojectinfo.org • Web site: www.financeprojectinfo.org

The Finance Project is a nonprofit policy research, technical assistance, and information organization created to help improve outcomes for children, families, and communities nationwide. WIN, a division of the Finance Project, is a clearinghouse for information, policy analysis, and technical assistance related to welfare, workforce development, and other human and community services. It produces a broad array of publications and information resources. Most are available online.

WOMEN'S ECONOMIC AGENDA PROJECT (WEAP)

449 Fifteenth St., 2nd Fl., Oakland, CA 94612
(510) 451-7379 • fax: (510) 986-8628
e-mail: weap@weap.org • Web site: www.weap.org

The Women's Economic Agenda Project seeks to give a voice to the poor. The organization utilizes rallies, town hall meetings, and in-classroom teaching methods to spread awareness about poverty, putting a strong emphasis on the plight of women suffering financially due to government policy making.

BOOKS

Judith Berk, *No Place to Be: Voices of Homeless Children*. Boston: Houghton Mifflin, 1992.

Joel Blau, *The Visible Poor: Homelessness in the United States*. New York: Oxford University Press, 1992.

Samuel Casey Carter, *No Excuse: Lessons from 21 High-Performing, High-Poverty Schools*. Washington, DC: Heritage Foundation, 2000.

Jason Deparle, *American Dream: Three Women, Ten Kids, and a Nation's Drive to End Welfare*. New York: Viking, 2004.

Greg J. Duncan and Jeanne Brooks-Gunn, *Consequences of Growing Up Poor*. New York: Russell Sage Foundation, 1999.

Kathryn Edin and Laura Lein, *Making Ends Meet: How Single Mothers Survive Welfare and Low-Wage Work*. New York: Russell Sage Foundation, 1997.

Sharon Hays, *Flat Broke with Children: Women in the Age of Welfare Reform*. New York: Oxford University Press, 2003.

Sharlene Janice Hesse-Biber and Gregg Lee Carter, *Working Women in America: Split Dreams*. New York: Oxford University Press, 2000.

Paul Jargowsky, *Poverty and Place: Ghettos, Barrios, and the American City*. New York: Russell Sage Foundation, 1997.

Christopher Jencks, *The Homeless*. Cambridge, MA: Harvard University Press, 1995.

Jennifer Johnson, *Getting By on the Minimum: The Lives of Working-Class Women*. New York: Routledge, 2002.

Caroline Knowles, *Bedlam on the Streets*. New York: Routledge, 2000.

Jonathan Kozol, *Rachel and Her Children: Homeless Families in America*. New York: Crown, 1988.

Sar A. Levitan et al., *Programs in Aid of the Poor.* Baltimore, MD: Johns Hopkins University Press, 2003.

Elliot Liebow, *Tell Them Who I Am: The Lives of Homeless Women.* New York: Penguin, 1995.

Garth L. Mangum, Stephen L. Mangum, and Andrew M. Sum, *The Persistence of Poverty in the United States.* Baltimore, MD: Johns Hopkins University Press, 2003.

Kathrine S. Newman, *No Shame in My Game: The Working Poor in the Inner City.* New York: Vintage, 2000.

Mark Robert Rank, *One Nation, Underprivileged: Why American Poverty Affects Us All.* New York: Oxford University Press, 2004.

Peter H. Rossi, *Down and Out in America: The Origins of Homelessness.* Chicago: University of Chicago Press, 1991.

Jeffrey Sachs, *The End of Poverty: Economic Possibilities for Our Time.* New York: Penguin, 2005.

Stephanie B. Seager, *Street Crazy: America's Mental Health Tragedy.* Redondo Beach, CA: Westcom, 2000.

David K. Shipler, *The Working Poor: Invisible in America.* New York: Knopf, 2004.

Beth Shulman, *The Betrayal of Work: How Low-Wage Jobs Fail 30 Million Americans and Their Families.* New York: New Press, 2003.

David A. Snow and Leon Anderson, *Down on Their Luck: A Study of Homeless Street People.* Berkeley: University of California Press, 1993.

Michael D. Tanner, *The Poverty of Welfare: Helping Others in the Civil Society.* Washington, DC: Cato Institute, 2003.

Jennifer Toth, *The Mole People: Life in the Tunnels Beneath New York City.* Chicago: Chicago Review, 1993.

Elizabeth Warren and Amelia Warren Tyagi, *The Two-Income Trap: Why Middle-Class Mothers and Fathers Are Going Broke.* New York: Basic Books, 2003.

William Julius Williams, *When Work Disappears: The World of the New Urban Poor.* New York: Vintage, 1996.

PERIODICALS

Brian J. Atwood and Michael Barnett, "Reduce Poverty—Get a Safer World," *Christian Science Monitor*, November 18, 2004.

Eleanor J. Bader, "Homeless on Campus," *Progressive*, July 2004.

Penelope Bennett, "So Difficult, So Painful," *New Statesman*, December 13, 2004.

Business Week, "Minimum Wage: The States Get It," November 29, 2004.

Economist, "Making Poverty History," December 18, 2004.

Liza Featherstone, "Down and Out in Discount America," *Nation*, January 3, 2005.

Ronald F. Ferguson, "The Working Poverty Trap: Low-Wage America, Two Views," *Public Interest*, Winter 2005.

Thomas Fisher, "When the Homeless Build Makeshift Shelters They Endanger Themselves and the Public at Large: Why Aren't Architects Doing More to Help?" *Architecture*, July 2004.

Lisa Freeman, "Squatting and the City," *Canadian Dimension*, November/December 2004.

Global Agenda, "The Other Planet: Poverty in America—How the Other 12.5% Live," August 31, 2004.

David R. Jones, "A First Line Against Homelessness," *New York Amsterdam News*, August 5, 2004.

Amy Joyner, "Improving Housing on Montana's Indian Reservations," *Montana Business Quarterly*, Autumn 2003.

Ronald Kohl, "Children in Poverty," *Machine Design*, November 4, 2004.

William Levernier, "An Analysis of Poverty in the American South: How Are Metropolitan Areas Different from Nonmetropolitan Areas?" *Contemporary Economic Policy*, July 2003.

Daniel T. Lichter and Martha L. Crowley, "Poverty in America: Beyond Welfare Reform—America's Poor," *Population Bulletin*, June 2002.

Karen Lowry Miller, "Juggling Two Worlds," *Newsweek*, November 29, 2004.

Richard Nadler, "Always with Us . . . and Wrong About the Poor," *National Review*, November 6, 2000.

National Catholic Reporter, "Hungry in America," February 15, 2002.

———, "Small Deeds Do Good," November 19, 2004.

New York Times, "Give Until It Stops Hurting," November 3, 2004.

———, "Shhh, Don't Say 'Poverty,'" November 22, 2004.

Eyal Press, "Straight Down the Middle," *Nation*, November 8, 2004.

Anna Quindlen, "A New Kind of Poverty," *Newsweek*, December 1, 2003.

Mark Robert Rank, "The Effects of Poverty on America's Families: Assessing Our Research Knowledge," *Journal of Family Issues*, October 2001.

Jonathan Rauch, "Forget Have's and Have-Not's: Think Do's and Do-Not's," *National Journal*, September 20, 2003.

Anastasia R. Snyder and Diane K. McLaughlin, "Female-Headed Families and Poverty in Rural America," *Rural Sociology*, March 2004.

Jim Wallis, "Rolling to Overcome Poverty," *Sojourners Magazine*, December 2004.

James D. Wolfensohn, "Fight Terrorism by Ending Poverty: America's Might—What to Do with It," *New Perspectives Quarterly*, Spring 2002.

Bill Wolpin, "The Fat and the Hungry: America's Growing Hunger and Poverty Problem," *American City & County*, January 1, 2004.

Seattle Housing And Resource
  Effort (SHARE), 87–91
self-reliance, 19, 24–25, 88–90
shoplifting
  by children, 41–42
  after court appearance, 45–46
  court sentencing for, 43–45
  in order to survive, 42–43
  prison term for, 43
Snyder, Margaret, 23
South, the. *See* Mississippi Delta, the
Spinks, Jackie, 32
The Sticky Wicket: Poverty's Home
  Page (Web site), 24
substance use/abuse, 69
  by children, mother's fears on, 65
  homelessness and, 15–16
  hospital treatment for, 85–86
  by Mexican migrant workers, 69
  by shoplifter, 44

teenager, poverty experienced by,
  47–50
Treanor, John, 44, 45

U.S. Census Bureau, 8

VanderStaay, Steven, 63, 87
veterans, homeless, 16

Wackerman, Daniel T., 92
welfare
  after divorce, 76
  for a family, 48
  in the Mississippi Delta, 54–55
  stigma of, 77
West Virginia, 9
Wilson, Pete, 23
working poor, the
  bonding among secretaries and,
    77–78
  child care issues of, 60–61
  expenses of, 76–77
  housing for, 66–67
  life story of, 75–76
  living conditions of, 60
  minimum wage job for, 63–64
  parental concerns about children
    among, 65–66
  working conditions of, 58–60,
    61–62, 64, 72–73, 74
  see also migrant workers
World War II, 19
Wright, Joe Louis, 43